anything but typical

ANYTHING but typical

NORA RALEIGH BASKIN

SIMON & SCHUSTER BOOKS FOR YOUNG READERS
New York London Toronto Sydney

also by nora raleigh baskin

The Truth About My Bat Mitzvah

for Steve

SIMON & SCHUSTER BOOKS FOR YOUNG READERS
An imprint of Simon & Schuster Children's Publishing Division
1230 Avenue of the Americas, New York, New York 10020
This book is a work of fiction. Any references to historical events, real people, or real locales are
used fictitiously. Other names, characters, places, and incidents are products of the author's imagination,
and any resemblance to actual events or locales or persons, living or dead, is entirely coincidental.
Copyright © 2009 by Nora Raleigh Baskin
SIMON & SCHUSTER BOOKS FOR YOUNG READERS is a trademark of Simon & Schuster, Inc.
Book design by Drew Willis
The text for this book is set in Leaf and Weiss.
Manufactured in the United States of America
2 4 6 8 10 9 7 5 3 1
CIP data for this book is available from the Library of Congress.
ISBN-13: 978-1-4169-6378-3
ISBN-10: 1-4169-6378-2

Acknowledgments

I once again, have many people to thank for their help and support in writing this book.

First and foremost I give my love and thanks to my editor at S&S, Alexandra Cooper, whose is just the right combination intelligent and kind, cheerleader and coach.

To Robin Millay, one of my smartest, oldest, most generous (she buys me books for no reason at all!), and most encouraging friends, who read an early draft of this novel—and still encouraged me. And worked with me on this all along the way.

To Estée Klar-Wolfond, founder of the Autism Acceptance Project, who answered all my e-mails and then spoke to me (for a long time) on the phone, which turned everything around and helped me find my way into this story.

To Michael Moon, current president of the Autism Acceptance Project (TAAP.com), who read a slightly-later-than-first draft of this story and gave me the greatest praise: "I was touched by the book for I could relate back to my childhood." Coming from him, it meant the world to me.

To my "Children's authors who breakfast" breakfast group, thank-you both, Tony Abbott and Elise Broach.

To the amazing artist, James Gulliver Hancock, who "drew" Jason's words so perfectly.

And to Lizzy Bromley, book designer extraordinaire, who also happen to have found JGH in the first place.

Chapter One

Most people like to talk in their own language.

They strongly prefer it. They so strongly prefer it that when they go to a foreign country they just talk louder, maybe slower, because they think they will be better understood. But more than *talking* in their own language, people like to hear things in a way they are most comfortable. The way they are used to. The way they can most easily relate to, as if that makes it more real. So I will try to tell this story in that way.

And I will tell this story in first person.

I not *he*. *Me* not *him*. *Mine* not *his*.

In a neurotypical way.

I will try—

To tell my story in their language, in your language.

I am Jason Blake.

And this is what someone would say, if they looked at me but could only see and could only hear in their own language:

That kid is weird (he's in SPED, you know). He blinks his eyes, sometimes one at a time. Sometimes both together. They open and close, open and close, letting the light in, shutting it out. The world blinks on and off.

And he flaps his hands, like when he is excited or just before he is going to say something, or when he is thinking. He does that the most when he's on the computer or reading a book. When his mind is focused on the words, it separates from his body, his body that almost becomes a burden, a weight.

Weight.

Wait.

Only his fingers don't stand still while they wait. They flap at the ends of his hands, at the ends of his wrists.

Like insects stuck on a string, stuck in a net. Like maybe they want to fly away. Maybe he does too.

In first grade they put a thick, purple rubber band across the bottom bar of his desk chair, so Jason would have something to jiggle with his feet when he was supposed to be sitting still. In second grade Matthew Iverson sent around a note saying, *If you think Jason Blake is a retard, sign this*, and Matthew got sent to the principal's office, which only made things worse for Jason.

In third grade Jason Blake was diagnosed with ASD, autistic spectrum disorder. But his mother will never use that term. She prefers three different letters: NLD, nonverbal learning disorder. Or these letters: PDD-NOS, pervasive developmental disorder–non-specific. When letters are put together, they can mean so much, and they can mean nothing at all.

From third grade until this year, sixth grade, Jason had a one-on-one aide, who followed him around school all day. She weighed two hundred and three pounds. (Jason asked her once, and she told him.) You couldn't miss seeing her.

But the thing people see the most is his silence, because some kinds of silence are actually visible.

When I write, I can be heard. And known.

But nobody has to look at me. Nobody has to see me at all.

School doesn't always go very well. It is pretty much a matter of time before the first thing of the day will go wrong.

But today I've gotten far. It is already third period. Mrs. Hawthorne is absent and so we are going to the library instead of art class. This is a good sign. You'd think art class would be one of the easiest classes, but it's not. I mean, it's not that it's hard like math, but it's hard like PE. A lot of space and time that is not organized.

Anything can go wrong in that kind of space.

But not in the library. There are computers in the library. And books. And computers. Keyboards and screens and desks that are built inside little compartments so you don't have to look at the person sitting next to you. And they can't look at me.

When we get into the library, somebody is already sitting in my seat, at my computer. At the one I want. Now I can't breathe. I want to log on to my Storyboard website. I was thinking about it all the way here. I have already had to wait so long. I don't know.

"Jason, this one is free," the lady says. She puts her hands on my shoulders. This lady is a lady I should know, but her face looks like a lot of other faces I don't know so well, and I group them all together. Her face is pinched, but her eyes are big, round like circles. Her hair doesn't move, like it's stuck in a ball. She belongs in the library or the front office or my dentist's office.

But she is here now, so I will assume she is the librarian.

I know from experience that she is trying to help me, but it doesn't. I can feel her weight on my shoulders like metal cutting my body right off my head. This is not a good thing.

I also know she wants me to look at her.

Neurotypicals like it when you look them in the eye. It is supposed to mean you are listening, as if the reverse were true, which it is not: Just because you are not looking at someone does not mean you are not listening. I can listen better when I am not distracted by a person's face:

What are their eyes saying?

Is that a frown or a smile?

Why are they wrinkling their forehead or lifting their cheeks like that? What does that mean?

How can you listen to all those words when you have to think about all that stuff?

But I know I will get in trouble if I don't look at the lady's eyes. I can force myself. I turn my head, but I will look at her sideways.

I know the right words to use.

Last year Jane, my one-on-one, taught me to say, "I am okay just as I am."

I am okay just as I am.

She told me I had to say something in this sort of situation. She said that people expect certain things. She said that people will misunderstand me if I don't say something.

This is one of the many, many things I need to run through in my mind, every time. Also the things my OT, my occupational therapist, has taught me:

Look people in the eye when you are talking (even if this makes it harder for you to listen).

Talk, even when you have nothing to say (that's what NTs do all the time).

Try to ignore everything else around you (even when those things may be very important).

If possible put your head and your body back together and try very hard not to shake or flap or twirl or twitch (even if it makes you feel worse to do this).

Don't blink.

Don't click your teeth. (These are the things people don't like. These are the things they hear but can't hear).

"I am okay just as I am," I say, and I take a step forward. I want the librarian to take her hands off my shoulders. The weight of her hands is almost unbearable, like lead. Like the lead apron the dentist puts on you when you get an x-ray, a crushing rock while the technician counts to ten. And you can't move.

Or they will have to do it all over again.

Also, I want to stand close, so there will be no confusion that I am next in line. The person at the computer turns around to the sound of my voice. It is a girl. Most girls look the same, and I can't tell one from the other.

Long hair. Earrings. Different tone of voice.

A Girl.

I don't know who this girl is, or if she already hates me, but chances are she does.

The girl doesn't say anything, so I have to look at her face and figure it out. Her eyes are squinched up, and her lips are pressed so tightly together they almost disappear. I recognize that she is unhappy or even angry, but I don't know why.

"You are breathing on me," she says. "You're so gross."

"Gross" could mean big or refer to a measurement or weight, but in this case it doesn't. It means she doesn't like me. She is, in fact, repulsed by me, which is how most girls react. My mom tells me not to worry. My mom tells me I will find a girlfriend one day, just like everyone else. I will find someone who sees how "special" I am. I know no girl will ever like me. No matter what I do, no matter how hard I try.

But maybe I am wrong.

I hope so.

I hope I am wrong and my mother is right. But usually I am right about these things.

"I was here first, Miss Leno," the girl says.

Miss Leno is the librarian's name.

"Jason, here," Miss Leno is saying. "Sit here. You can use this computer."

But I can't use that computer. I don't want to. I can't. My breathing is too loud inside my ears. I stiffen my body, solidify my weight, so she can't move me with her hands. You'd be surprised at how quickly people will try to move you with their hands when they don't get what they want with their words.

I wish Jane were here with me right now and then this wouldn't happen. Words don't always work.

"Jason, hold still. There's no need to get so upset. There are plenty of other computers."

Miss Leno is trying to shift my weight off my feet, and she's trying to pretend she's not, as if she's just walking with me, instead of pushing me, which is what she's doing.

"Jason, please." But she doesn't mean *please*. There is no *please* in anything Miss Leno is asking. She is pulling me.

I feel off balance, like I am going to fall. I need to shift my weight back and forth, back and forth, rock to stabilize myself. I can feel my chance to use my computer getting further and further away from me. There isn't even enough time left in the period. I might not get to log on at all, even if this girl does get up. A hundred little pieces threaten to come apart.

"Jason, please, calm down. Calm down." Miss Leno's voice sounds like a Xerox machine.

Sometimes there is nothing to hold me together.

Chapter Two

There are some writers who know things and post them on the Internet so other writers can learn them. Some of them say that there are only seven plots in the whole world:

Man vs nature.

Man vs man.

Man vs environment.

Man vs machine.

Man vs the supernatural.

Man vs self.

Man vs religion.

It could be a woman, too, but they just say "man" in order to make it easier for themselves. Because they all seem to be able to understand it, because they are only speaking in their own language. In an NT language.

But I can do that too.

When I try.

Very hard.

It means man or woman vs nature.

Man or woman vs man or woman.

And so on.

Other writers say there are only three plots: happy ending, unhappy ending, and literary plot (that's the kind of ending that is uncertain). There is a whole book called *Twenty Master Plots*, which I happen to own. And another author wrote that he thought there were thirty-nine plots.

But really, if you ask me, there is only one kind of plot.

One.

Stuff happens.

That's it.

This is what happens next:

"C'mon, Maggie, get up. Give him that computer. You're not even doing anything."

Now Aaron Miller is standing behind me. Me, who is behind the girl who is using my computer. Miss Leno, behind both of us, still has her hands on my shoulders. If she doesn't let go, I don't know what will happen.

But stuff usually always happens.

I have known Aaron Miller since kindergarten, from back when I was the same as everyone else. You might not even have picked me out of a crowd. Nobody was very good at anything back then, and a lot of kids did weird things and didn't know enough to hide them. Charlie Karl wet his pants seven times that year. Chelsea Grey got caught sneaking into the cubbies and stealing the meat out of all the sandwiches she could find. Liza Duchamps picked her nose and ate it during circle time. Now that same girl is running for sixth-grade class president.

Aaron Miller was my friend in kindergarten. I'd like to say he still is, but by definition I can't. He hasn't come to my house in five years. He hasn't invited me to his birthday party since second grade. I am pretty certain I am not on Aaron Miller's buddy list, even though he is on mine. But he is always nice to me, and when I sit at his table at lunch, he will talk to me.

He doesn't get angry when I don't talk back the same way.

"Anyway, you're not supposed to be playing games on the computer, Maggie," Aaron says to the girl. The girl's name is Maggie.

"What is it your business?" the girl, Maggie, says, but she stops her typing and looks at Aaron.

"Everything is my business, Maggie," Aaron says. "And you're just being stubborn. You're being mean."

Maggie says, "I'm not mean." She immediately signs off and closes the window she has open on the screen. Then Maggie takes her fingers off the keyboard and pushes her chair back. It screeches, but I don't move out of the way. I might be mistaken about what she is doing.

I'm not.

"All yours, Jay-Man," Aaron says.

But there are only twenty-three minutes left in the period.

"Ow," Maggie says, but I know I didn't do anything that could have hurt her. I am just sitting down. She is just standing up.

I want to say thank you to Aaron, but I need to claim my seat first, just in case someone else comes over and takes my turn from me. That has happened many times before. And then all this work would have been for nothing. I need to open my website, because the computers at school are slow, and this will take time too. The sooner you can begin something, the sooner it is done.

I am logging in.

"That is very nice of you, Maggie," I hear Miss Leno saying. "I am sure Jason appreciates it very much."

The Storyboard home page rolls on to the screen, bit by bit, from the top down. I had to get special permission to go to this website. My mother had to write a letter and even the principal, Dr. T., had to approve. And then the librarian, who was not Miss Leno, but the one before her, unblocked the site for me. The school had to validate that all Storyboard users are under seventeen and that the site is monitored. There is a Storyboard site for adults. But that one is completely separate.

Now all I need to do is type in my screen name and password. But Miss Leno has not walked away the way she should. She is still standing nearby. Usually she walks around the library asking kids if they need help, or she sits behind her desk and checks out books. Or goes into the back room and I don't know what they do back there, but I wish she would go now.

I will focus on my Storyboard screen name and password. There are only twenty-two minutes left in this period, and I need to see if I got a response to my last posting. Miss Leno makes a scratchy sound from her throat while the final graphics for my website start to load on the screen. She has still not walked away.

I am trying to remember my list of the things a person could want but doesn't tell you what it is. Sometimes they just want to say something, and they are waiting for you to look at them before they will say it. That is often the case. But Miss Leno was already doing a lot of talking without me looking at her, so that's probably not it.

Sometimes people stand around when they are waiting for you to do or say something. Something they think you *should* do or say. So they just wait, like that's going to help you understand what it is they want you to say or do.

It doesn't.

"And I am sure Jason wants to say thank you, don't you, Jason?" Miss Leno finally gets it out.

I want so badly to check my story posting.

I am very grateful that Aaron helped me to get on my computer, but now I just really want to view my website, and I don't understand what Miss Leno wants me to do. I can't say thank you to Aaron; he is not here anymore. I can hear his voice. He is all the way across the room by the card catalog now, and if

I get up, I could lose my computer all over again. Does she want me to say thank you to Maggie? Maggie doesn't want me to talk to her. Even Miss Leno must know that. Besides, she didn't *want* to get up and give me the computer. She just didn't want Aaron not to like her.

All I need to do is log on and scroll down to my entry. If someone has written to me, there will be a number next to my name. All I can do is keep my eyes on the screen.

"Well, Mr. Blake. Showing a little appreciation would go a long way with your fellow classmates," Miss Leno says. Her voice is angry, but she is walking away.

Showing?

How do you *show* appreciation? Appreciation is an emotion. It's a feeling. You can't draw a picture of it. Why do people want everyone to act just like they do? Talk like they do. Look like they do. Act like they do.

And if you don't—

If you don't, people make the assumption that you do not *feel* what they feel.

And then they make the assumption—

That you must not feel anything at all.

Chapter Three

Every morning I get up, a word pops into my head, usually just before breakfast.

Just before breakfast and right after I brush my teeth. Or just *as* I am brushing my teeth. Sometimes I know what the word means, and sometimes I don't.

I say it out loud.

It could be a hard word or it could be an easy one.

This morning it is "confluence." I watch myself in the mirror, and I hear the word "confluence." I am not sure what "confluence" means. I have an idea, but I am not sure. I think it has something to do with coming together. *A confluence of ideas*. I think I have heard that expression.

I say it out loud.

"Confluence."

I am looking in the mirror and I am thinking that if I didn't talk and I didn't move, if I held my hands at my sides and stood very straight, I'd look like any other twelve-year-old boy. My hair is short and dark. My eyes are nicely formed and light brown in color. My mouth is normal. My lips, an even shape. My skin is good. My teeth are white. My ears don't stick out, and I know they are clean, even though I can't see them. I clean them every day.

Confluence, like two rivers coming together.

I am like a leaf on a river, riding along the top of the water, not quite floating, not quite drowning. So I can't stop, and I can't control the direction I am going. I can feel the water, but I never know which way I am heading.

But I might feel lucky this day and avoid the sticks and branches scratching and pulling at me.

My dad tells me there is no such thing as luck, good or bad.

My dad is the guy who puts the words up on the television while you are watching a basketball game, or a football game, or sometimes baseball. He sits in a trailer outside the arena or the stadium or the field and watches everything on a screen while he types into a computer. He puts up the score, the names, the stats, and interesting facts that his producer tells him to. So he watches a lot of sports.

And he says there is no such thing as luck.

Life is what you make of it, my dad says.

My mother is a different story. That is an expression, since she herself is not really a story. Being able to understand abstract expressions like that is a sign of intelligence. IQ tests are filled with them. Like "People in glass houses shouldn't throw stones" or "A penny saved is a penny earned." Part of the scoring on the test depends on how well you can understand and interpret those sayings.

Lots of neurotypicals don't even understand them. But I do.

My mother wants to help me. She wants me to be happy. And I think my mother wants to fix me. She wants me to be more like her, even though she doesn't seem so happy a lot of the time.

And if she can't fix me, at least she wants to explain how I got like this.

So she is looking for a reason. A reason to explain me.

It could be:

The mercury in the DPT vaccines

A wayward chromosome

A mutated gene

Too much peanut butter eaten during the first trimester

Not enough oxygen during delivery

Not enough peanut butter (is there such a thing?)

Smoking during pregnancy (but my mother didn't smoke)

Maybe it's the air pollution, or the fertilizers in the vegetables, or hormones in the milk, acid rain, global warming. Maybe it's rays coming out of the television. Or the microwave.

Or maybe it is just me.

One of the two responses to my story is from someone who calls themselves Nique79, which I think might be like Nick or even Nickie, but people like to spell things differently online. Because maybe your real name, the way you spell it, is already taken.

My story is about a man, the story I posted on the Storyboard website under the category Miscellaneous, which is where you post anything that is not true fan fiction. All my stories are original.

The majority of the fan fiction postings are continuations or retellings of someone else's story, or even movies or television shows, like *Harry Potter*. Or *Star Wars*. Or *CSI*. Or *Pirates of the Caribbean*. And *The Gilmore Girls*.

But my stories are all original, so they don't get as many hits.

My story is about a man.

I wrote a story about a man who can't talk because he has a giant tumor growing in his throat. He was born with it, but nobody knows that, so they just think he's really stupid and that he doesn't have anything to say. So he lives alone at the edge of his village, where he carves fantastic figures out of wood, like little bears juggling and fish jumping up out of the water, sailing through the air, a tiny hummingbird drinking from a flower, and then he carves a little boy for himself to have as a friend. Even though, of course, the wooden boy can't talk either.

I know I borrowed a little from the Pinocchio idea, and I hope nobody will notice that. But they don't have a Pinocchio category anyway. I click to open the first comment on my story.

Nique79 writes, `Great story. Keep writing.`

The second comment is from PhoenixBird, but I decide to wait until I get home from school to open it. It is like saving the last piece of candy from your Halloween bag, which you shouldn't do, because it gets hard and sticks to the wrapper, and even if you can pick all the paper off the slimy candy when you try to eat it, it hurts and gets caught in your teeth for a really long time.

But that's probably not what I really mean, since eating old Halloween candy doesn't sound good at all.

Chapter Four

There is no explanation for my little brother, Jeremy.

There doesn't seem to be a word or label or reason for what he is.

He simply is.

He is a typical neurotypical, which means he's never had an aide in school, and when he wants something or doesn't want something, nobody seems to have a problem understanding what it is. And even though he is only nine years old, he is better than me at figuring out what other people want from him. On the other hand he is afraid of bananas, and from when he was two and a half until about last year, Jeremy refused to wear sandals. He would kick and scream until his toes were safe inside a clean pair of socks and solid shoes. But nobody thought too much about that. Some of the weird things he does my mother says are "modeled behavior," which is just another way of saying he learned them from me.

Like his temper.

And some of the things Jeremy does that have nothing to do with me get blamed on me anyhow.

Like how he won't eat any food on his plate that has touched any other food on his plate. So my mother bought these dishes with separate compartments and said they were for me. But it was always Jeremy who couldn't take a forkful of his potatoes without getting them all over his meat.

Not me.

He does do a lot of talking, but that doesn't mean anything. Because even though it is harder for me to talk than to listen, and even though it is also hard for me to listen, I think it is much harder for NTs to listen than it is to talk. This is something I have observed over the years.

When Jeremy was born, everyone was afraid I would hurt him. My mother would carry him down to the basement with her when she did the laundry, and she carried him in his little baby seat into the bathroom with her when she took a shower. Maybe she thought I didn't notice.

But I did.

And whenever they *did* let me hold him, someone was always right next to me. My grandmother, whose hands shake more than mine, would keep her arm right under the baby, even when I was sitting down and they put him on my lap.

My grandmother always shouts at me when she talks, like she thinks I am hard of hearing, which is completely the opposite. I hear very, very well. My grandmother smells like chemicals and fake flowers. I know my grandmother when I smell her. I don't like to look at her face. But I can tell it's her, every time. I don't like her very much.

"You are so good with your new little brother. I can tell you love him very much," my grandmother said that day. She said each word very slowly and very loudly.

That was the first time I really understood what a lie was.

I barely knew my new little brother. He didn't do anything. I didn't love him. He pooped in his diaper and then he smelled. And he cried, so I'd have to put my hands over my ears as tight as I could.

I knew what love was.

It was how I felt it sometimes when I was with my mother. The way I would sometimes feel just my head or sometimes just my toes and they'd feel warm. And I felt safe with my mother. I could breathe easily. I knew I didn't love my new little brother.

But my daddy told me I would.

Soon, he told me. Soon Jeremy would be my best friend. He would want to play with me more than anyone else in the world.

He would let me share all his toys, and he would laugh when I made a joke. My dad was teaching me some good jokes to tell.

"Soon" meant I had to wait another month until Jeremy could even smile and another ten months at least until he would be able to walk. And then he would probably follow me around the house and want to do everything I was doing.

But not yet.

All Jeremy did then was cry and poop and take up space in my mother's arms and make it hard for me to breathe.

I was looking at the skin at the top of Jeremy's head that you could see because he didn't have any hair. There was a tiny round hole in his skull that moved in and out. I wondered how he could do that. My mother said it's called a fontanelle and that all babies have one. But I wasn't sure about that.

He moved it up and down, in and out, in a perfect rhythm.

Maybe he was going to be really amazing. I just had to wait.

"Don't you, Jason?" Now my grandmother was talking even louder, which I already knew people would do when they thought I wasn't listening. But I was always listening, I just didn't have anything to say. "Don't you just love this little baby boy?"

My mother had told me I needed to answer when that happened. She had a little sign she'd make with her hands. I needed to say something, no matter how hard it was. If someone asks you a question, you are supposed to say something, especially if they ask it twice. Even though you'd think they'd get the hint the first time. I had already learned that if I concentrated on my mouth long enough, I could get the right words to come out. At least one right word. But most people don't wait long enough for the right words, so I opened my mouth.

"No," I said.

"You don't mean that. Of course you love your little brother," my grandmother said.

I said it again. "No."

That's when she took my baby brother off my lap.

Chapter Five

"Are you going to read your e-mails now?" Jeremy is asking me.

The best thing about Jeremy is that I don't ever have to answer him, not with words anyway. And I don't ever have to look him in the face. He doesn't even want me to. He likes to talk to me while he is watching TV or reading one of his comic books or biting his nails, which is what he is doing right now. He is very serious about biting his nails. My mom is always telling him to stop, so Jeremy doesn't ever do it when she can see him. That is one thing I really admire about my little brother. He is very tricky about biting his nails.

I want him to be a little more quiet about it, though. The clicking noise his teeth make on his fingernails bothers me.

My hands fly around my head.

I don't really think about doing this. It is more like my hands know what to do all by themselves. They know it makes my mind feel better.

"Oh, sorry," Jeremy says. And he stops. Or he tries to be more quiet about it, I am not sure which, because I keep my eyes on the screen. I am waiting for my Web pages to appear. It won't take long now that I am home. My computer is faster than the one in the library.

"So now, are you going to go on the Internet now?"

But the Internet is not really a place you can go.

It is not really a net at all, but it is the biggest, most complex place in the whole world. It hosts hundreds of languages, millions of words, billions and billions of bytes of information every single second. And similar to what goes into my brain and what comes out of my mouth, it is very hard to explain.

But I will try, because I love Jeremy. I tell him about my story on Storyboard.

"You are the best writer in the whole world, Jason." Jeremy is still talking. "I bet a hundred million people read your story and you are going to be a famous writer when you grow up."

Jeremy knows, because I told him, that probably very few people have viewed my story since I posted it last week and that only two people have written comments. But that is how Jeremy is. He doesn't think very much about the meaning of the words that come out of his mouth. It took me a long time and more careful observation to figure this out.

People don't mean everything they say, my mother has told me. So has my physical therapist.

Then why do they say it?

Why do people say things they don't really mean?

So far no one has given me a very good answer to that.

I click on my second response, the one from PhoenixBird, the one I was saving until I got home.

Now I am home.

`I feel I could have written your story. It is so beautiful. I have to go to cheerleading practice but I can't wait for your next story.`

I read it again. Sometimes the same words and letters can have different meanings, so you have to be careful.

"Why are you so quiet, Jason?"

Jeremy doesn't mean *quiet*. I am always quiet. He means *still*. I can feel my body sitting in this chair. I can feel my feet (inside my shoes, touching the floor) and my legs (flat on the edge of the seat), my head and my arms, my fingers (resting on the keyboard but not pressing down), all at the same time, which I usually can't do. And none of them is moving.

I am still.

I am completely still and I know it.

I read the comment one more time.

Because something tells me—

That this note is from a girl. There are some boy cheerleaders, but I don't think a boy would admit that.

So I think PhoenixBird is a girl.

So I think a girl has just said something nice to me.

Chapter Six

Last year for our summer vacation we went to New Jersey.

Jeremy really wanted to go to Disneyland, but we went to New Jersey. We stayed in a house on the beach. One afternoon Dad and Jeremy drove to Six Flags Great Adventure, because Dad said it was just like Disneyland. I didn't want to go. I don't like rides. I don't like bright lights. And I really don't like crowds and loud noise.

Six Flags really isn't anything like Disneyland, even Jeremy knew that.

"Sorry, Jason," my mother said after Jeremy and Dad left for Six Flags Great Adventure, which was really odd, because there wasn't any reason for her to be sorry for me. I didn't want to go. Unless she was really sorry for herself, which happens sometimes, but she'd never say that. She probably didn't like staying in our beach house playing Scrabble anymore. My mother isn't as good at Scrabble as I am.

She might be sorry about that.

"So how about you and I go out to a special restaurant?" my mother asked me.

We were in our rented house, but we had some stuff from home. We had our own sheets and pillows and blankets. Of course we brought our own Scrabble set. My mom also packed for me a plate, a glass, and silverware, so then Jeremy wanted his own from home too. Mom didn't want to, but Dad said we could make room in the car. But Mom was mad about it. I couldn't tell from her face, but she did shut the door really hard. So she could be sorry about that.

"So how 'bout it, Jason? Just you and me. Like old times," my mother said.

"Just like old times," I said.

It was easy sometimes to just say the last words I had heard when I knew she wanted me to say something. I knew my mother wanted something from me.

I knew every time, but there was nothing I could do. So sometimes she would cry. Sometimes she would just close her fists very tightly, squeeze her eyes shut, and that's when I could look at her. My mother's face is very beautiful, like hills of softness, and careful arches of tiny hair, and moving lips, white teeth.

We went to the Channel Marker restaurant, just me and my mother. Just like old times. My mother asked for a table in the farthest corner like we always do. But there was a wait. We had to wait.

Weight.

"We can wait, can't we, Jason?" my mother said. "Relax your face, Jason. Take out your book."

We sat down on a hard wooden bench and I started to read.

"Relax your face, Jason," my mother said. She put two fingers on the side of my head. We still waited. And I read my book that my mom always brings for me.

"Jason, I have to use the bathroom. I'll be right back. Stay here. Okay, Jason? Just stay here. I'll be right back."

I nodded again. I kept my eyes on my book, even though it was hard to concentrate.

It was noisy in the restaurant. Every time the door opened, I could hear cars driving on the road. I heard a dog bark outside, and I heard the wood floor creak when someone walked by the doorway to the kitchen.

My occupational therapist was teaching me how to try and block out all these sounds. She taught me to hear them one by one and then send them away.

Hear them. Hold them. And let them go.

Until, finally, all I saw were the words on the page and all I heard was my own breathing. And I knew I was calm.

I could wait.

I kept reading. I knew I was calm, and I was proud of myself. My mother would come back from the bathroom, and I would not be blinking or flapping or rocking. I would be reading, and no one would know any different. No one would have to see me.

I heard two pairs of feet come close. And then girls' voices.

"Ask him. Come on, ask him."

"No. You ask him."

I kept my head down, but I let my eyes leave my book to the shoes. The girls' shoes on the floor. Two girls. And then a hand. A girl's hand.

It waved at me.

At me?

I could look up and then down again. It was a girl, her mouth turned up, her teeth showing. Her eyes were directed right at me. I wasn't sure what she was trying to say, but I knew she wanted something.

Did I know her?

Was this someone I was supposed to know?

Sometimes I have trouble recognizing people I am supposed to know. Especially if there is nothing for me to use as a clue, like a particular kind of hair, very long or very straight or very black, in combination with something else, like a beard or glasses or being very fat, or braces on their teeth. Or where they are when I see them, like the doctor's office or the gas station or the library.

Sometimes someone's voice, a hat they always wear, who they are with, or their perfume can help.

I wished my mother would come back. She would know who these girls were. She would talk to them. I looked in the direction she walked away. There were so many people, so many legs, and so much noise.

What am I supposed to do?

"You think he's cute—you ask him."

"Katie!"

"He didn't hear me. Ask him."

I *did* hear them. I heard them and then I understood. But it was too late. I tried to think of everything I was supposed to do. But it was too late. The button of my jeans was poking me in the stomach, and the collar of my shirt was rubbing on my neck. The lights from the ceiling were hurting my eyes. There was a horrible smell coming from a tray that went by.

I knew.

The girl was waving at me, I thought. *She wants to be my friend. She thinks I am cute.*

Cute. No one had ever called me cute before, other than my mother. No one. I knew what it meant now.

But it was too late.

"Why is he doing that?"

Doing what? What was I doing? I know what I am doing. I can feel it but I can't stop. It's too late.

"Ew, Katie. Look."

"Is he smiling at you?"

"Ew, no. It's just his face. Let's go."

They stood up. The girls' shoes and the girls' voices. The voices were whispers now, but they were louder. I could hear them. The shoes were moving away.

"Ew, gross. He's so weird. Move, Katie. Well, move faster."

A couple of days later it occurred to me what had happened, and what it meant and what it would mean to me forever.

I thought then, my mother was wrong about me and girls, and growing up and having a normal life. About finding someone who thinks I'm different *special*.

About having a girlfriend.

Until just now.

Until I got an e-mail from PhoenixBird.

Who's definitely a girl.

Chapter Seven

PhoenixBird wrote a story, and she asked me to read it before she posts it. I read it, but I don't answer her right away. I know she can't tell if I've received her e-mail or read her story. There is no way to check status on this website. Maybe she will think I am away on vacation and can't get to my computer. Or our power was out. There are many reasons a person hasn't checked their favorite website. It could be anything.

It makes me feel a little bit like I am lying, but I need more time.

PhoenixBird's story is set in the future, but it isn't science fiction. You can just tell it isn't science fiction. It's something different.

There are basically two types of fiction, literary and genre. Science fiction would be one type of genre fiction, but there are so many, like mysteries, western novels, crime novels, fantasy. And romance.

Genre is kind of like how you know what is going to happen in a particular kind of book. In a crime story you know you are going to learn who the bad guy is, but he may or may not get caught. In a mystery you want the mystery to be solved. In fantasy there has to be magic, maybe even vampires or werewolves.

Romance goes like this:

Boy gets girl.

Boy loses girl.

Boy gets girl again.

The end.

It can't be any other way.

PhoenixBird's story doesn't seem to fit into any of these categories. It is about a world where every single person lives in their own apartment—everyone, every man and woman and even the children. The children seem to come into the world pretty much self-sufficient, so they can already walk and talk and take care of themselves. This saves a lot of time and money. It's not that the people are all the same in this world, but they are all equal. No one has to rely or lean or depend on anyone else.

In PhoenixBird's story everybody has food and clothing. No one is ever cold or hungry or homeless. All illness has been cured. No one ever gets sick and needs a doctor. Nobody needs any help doing anything. And she doesn't write this, but I am guessing that no one feels left out, because no one *is* left out.

In the story the world is perfect: Nobody needs anybody else.

Adjudicate.

That's the word that came into my mind this morning. I think I know what it means, or I can figure it out. Usually you can figure out a word by its place in a sentence or by breaking it down. I see the word "judge" in "adjudicate."

"Adjudicate."

I watch my mouth in the mirror.

I wonder if I am pronouncing it correctly.

I don't know where this word came from, but I will carry it with me today. It's Saturday. My parents' date night is tonight.

"Chicken nuggets are all ready on the tray, Suzy," my mother says.

I know Suzy has already seen the chicken nuggets on top of the stove. I watched her turn on the oven to three hundred fifty degrees, so she knows.

"Just turn on the oven for a couple of minutes before you want to cook them," my mother says. She has lipstick on, and she straightened her curly hair. The first time she did that, I cried when I saw her. And then I ran over and tried to pull her hair from her head. It didn't look like her, and I got scared. Now I am used to it, even though I think it looks like she is wearing a wig.

"Jeremy needs to be in bed by nine. He has to brush his teeth, and he can read one book. Then it's lights out," my mother is saying. Then she turns to me.

My mother used to put me to bed every night. She used to lie right next to me under my covers and tell me a story. She would lie with me until I fell asleep. I could smell her hair and feel the heat that came off her body. *Let your arms go,* my mother would say. *Let your hands be still. Let your face rest. Let your feet rest.* One body part at a time, and I would close my eyes and know she was not going to leave me, so I could fall asleep.

But then she said I got too old. I needed to go to bed by myself.

"Jason can . . ." She doesn't finish her sentence.

"We will be fine, Mrs. Blake," Suzy said. "You two get going. It's late."

"Jason can take care of himself now," my mother went on. My dad is standing by the door. He has his coat on, which means he is ready to leave. His hands are in his pockets, and I can hear his car keys jingling, which means he is worried about being late.

"I'm here to help, Mrs. Blake. Jason and I go back a long way," Suzy says. She is waving my parents toward the door with her hands.

Suzy has never made me feel stupid. She never seems uncomfortable around me. She has been babysitting for us since I was very little, since just after Jeremy was born. Her kids are all grown, she told me. When Suzy talks, she uses her hands a lot. I can look at her hands, and they say more than her words.

Right now Suzy's hands are saying: *I like Jason.*

Still, when my mom and dad head to the door, my brain starts to buzz. It fills up and lifts off my body. When I was little, I think I believed it really did lift off my body, or at least I didn't know it *hadn't*. Now I know better. I want to reach up and touch my head, because even though my brain knows my head is still attached, my body has stopped believing me.

I have to remember that I am breathing. In and out. Listen to the sound it makes in my nose and my ears. My chest goes up with the sound. I am supposed to notice this. It is supposed to help connect my head back to my body before my hands can fly away. My mother doesn't like it when my hands fly away.

I keep my eyes away from the door and my mom and dad and the feeling I will have when they leave. Suzy has told me it is homesickness, even though I am home. Suzy says it means I love my parents very much and I don't want them to leave.

I have to breathe.

My dad comes over and kisses the top of my head. "Have fun with Suzy," my dad says. "We will be home before you know it."

I know what he means. He doesn't want me to feel scared.

My dad smells like the cologne that I bought him for Father's Day last year. That makes me feel good, like we are connected. I try to slow down my breathing. I can feel the heaviness of his head on the top of my head when he kisses me, so even though I don't watch him walk back to the door, I can still feel it, and we are connected.

I hear the door open.

"Good-bye, Jason. Be good," my mom is calling out. I hear Jeremy running up to the door.

"Bye, Mom. Bye, Dad," Jeremy says. His voice sounds muffled, because he probably has his face stuffed into my dad's coat. I don't know how he can do that. That makes it harder to breathe.

"I love you," he says.

The music on the television. The refrigerator ice maker shuts off. My dad's keys get louder. Jeremy's voice. He is upset about something. Something about cookies. The sounds from outside. A car. The door must be open.

I have to breathe. I know they will be back, because I am breathing.

If PhoenixBird's story were real, I am thinking, *I would live alone and so I could not ever be homesick.* That would be good. My head wouldn't be buzzing. I could breathe easily.

I know my mother worries that I won't be able to live alone. *Not now,* she says, *but someday,* she says, *someday you will want to.* But I don't. So it would be good if PhoenixBird's story were real. If I lived in her story.

But it wouldn't be good, because I love my mother and father, and that is why I am homesick even while I am home.

If I lived in the story, I wouldn't need my mother. I wouldn't be homesick when she goes out. And she'd be happy.

"I know. I know, Carl." It's my mother's voice, which is outside the door and the door is still open. She is not happy now. She wants me to act like Jeremy does when he is homesick. He runs up and smothers his face, but I couldn't breathe if I did that. That's what she wants. I know that.

But I wouldn't be able to breathe.

A car drives by. My mother's shoes are on the wooden steps and now on the pavement. My dad coughs.

"Stop it, Liz. Jason loves you very much. You know he does," my dad says. His hand is on the metal door handle.

"If you say so," my mother says.

The door swings shut.

But if we lived in PhoenixBird's story, my mother wouldn't be so sad.

I know PhoenixBird is waiting to hear what I think of her story, but I am afraid. When I was little, I used to think that there was actually someone watching me when I typed into the computer, because it responded so quickly. Or that someone was actually inside. The first time I got an instant message, I ran to the window to see who was there, who could know I was at my computer.

Who could know what I was doing?

And even though I know better now, a part of me still worries. I still worry that someone is there. That if I type into my computer, if I answer PhoenixBird, she will be able to see me.

Tonight I write back to PhoenixBird.

I have a few comments. There were little mistakes and a place I thought she could "show more" and not just "tell." I tell her it was like watching a television show, and you wouldn't want to just have a blank screen with a narrator telling you the story. Like that long, boring beginning of *Star Wars* with all the words moving across the screen. You want to see pictures.

It's really good, PhoenixBird, I write in my message to her.

I tell her I can hardly wait to read the ending.

Chapter Eight

Before I go to bed, I always get an hour of computer time. I have only seven minutes left tonight.

"Well, I'll be in to say good night," Suzy tells me. She stands in my doorway. "You're really good on that computer, aren't you?"

I look up at the ceiling of my room, where my dad has stenciled letters, the whole alphabet.

My dad painted my ceiling when I was four years old, when I first started spelling. I could spell anything then, anything I saw on a shampoo bottle, a road sign, a grocery bag. At first my mom and dad thought I was just copying the letters. And they thought it was great that I could form my letters in a straight line. Then they realized I could spell anything, not just copy. Anything I had seen, even once. They thought I was some kind of a genius.

So they told anybody and everybody who would listen.

At least my mom did.

I may have only been in nursery school, but I knew what was going on.

It was the old bait and switch routine.

"No, he isn't hard of hearing. Look, watch how he can write his letters. Jason can write his name and all our names, anything. And he's only four years old. Just *turned* four."

I had a blue plastic writing board with a magnetic pen that erased clean when you lifted it over your head and shook it back and forth.

"Of course he talks when he wants to. *And* he can spell."

McDonald's

Target

Closed

United States Postal Service

KitchenAid

Volkswagen

Aitoro's Appliance Store

"Why is he writing all those meaningless words?" my grandmother said, my genius apparently lost on her.

"Well, anyone can talk," my mother countered. "Just listen to Bobby's kid. He just won't shut up, will he?"

Bobby is my mother's brother, Uncle Bobby, and his "kid" is named Seth Zimmerman.

My dad is pretty quiet too. He talks, but most of the time

46

he listens. But that day I remember exactly what he said to my grandmother. And to my mother.

"It's not meaningless to Jason," my dad said.

"What? What's not meaningless?" My mother's face red and her eyes wet, even though she wasn't crying. She was hurting, even I could see that.

"I never said—," my grandmother started, but my dad interrupted her.

"The words. *And* the letters. Just because you don't understand their meaning doesn't mean they don't have one."

That afternoon my dad made my ceiling speak.

"Oh, my," Suzy says. "How is it I never noticed that before?"

I can tell by the sound that Suzy's neck must be bent all the way back, her voice bends with it. She is looking up too. She is not coming all the way into my room, but she is close. When I looked up, she looked up.

The letters of the alphabet don't move, but if I stare at them, some will become blurry and others will move forward, some become darker and others lighter, shades of the blue and red and yellow. I try to spell words, holding on to the letters in my mind and imagining their meaning. Or I can just look at their shapes, as if they had no sound of their own. Just arcs and curves and straight, very straight lines that will never touch but continue forever into infinity.

Some of the letters look like they came from the same family, tall and thin, and their children, the lowercase letters, look exactly like they do. Like *M*, and *N*, and *T*. Others have children that are nothing like their parents. Like they came from a whole other strand of DNA. So you can put the mother and her child right next to each other and they look nothing alike. Like *E*, and *A*, and *D*.

The big *D* and the little *D* face in completely opposite directions. They don't even look at each other. But they are related. They make the same sound.

They are a family.

Part of the whole family of the English alphabet—of letters that have resonance to make words that sound different in different mouths and have different meanings to different people. People even argue about words, and sentences, about speeches and books and letters.

People will say, *I didn't say that.* Or, *I didn't mean that.* And the other person will say, *Yes, you did. I heard you.*

You called me a name.

He told me he'd do that. Or this. But he didn't.

Use your words. Use your words.

They have to be said out loud?

I told you never to do that again.

But I did. And now I am in trouble.

Because I said so.

And there they are, all the twenty-six letters but forty-four sounds called phonemes. If you look closely, there are diphthongs and schwa sounds. Vowels, long and short. And consonants hard and soft. Some people talk in accents, so you would spell the very same word a very different way, if you were to spell it as it sounds.

To you.

Or you.

There are digraphs where two letters make one totally new sound, like *th* and *ch* and *sh*.

As in *Shush . . . Shush, I am looking at the letters on my ceiling.*

"Get ready to shut down your computer, okay, Jason? And get some sleep," Suzy says.

I rest my hands on my lap. They are tired. And when I lie down in my bed, I will stop rocking. It is late.

I want to tell Suzy good night. I want to tell her thank you for letting me breathe.

I want the letters to form words in my mouth, but they stay on the ceiling.

"I know, Jason," she says. "It's late, but I'm glad I got to see you."

Then, just as I am about to sign off, PhoenixBird writes me back right away.

She must be sitting at her computer too. Right at this minute, somewhere. She could live in Alaska or right here in

Connecticut. But either way she can't see me.

She says her story is for a school assignment and she really needs to bring up her language arts grade.

Thanks for the help, she writes. I already fixed it up and it's so much better. I hope I get a good grade. It is for a language arts assignment and I need to get a good grade. My parents are kind of on my case lately. So thanks!

PhoenixBird is worried about school.

Just like me.

By second grade most everyone had caught up to my alphabet and spelling abilities. I wasn't such a genius anymore, and by third grade I was behind in almost everything else: verbal skills, social performance, physical aptitude, and age-appropriate behavior. (I wasn't too good at controlling my temper either, but I am better now.)

The teachers started pressuring my mom to have me tested.

A year later the only letters anybody cared about were ASD, NLD, and maybe ADD or ADHD, which I think my mom would have liked better.

BLNT.

Better luck next time.
I just made that up.

Maybe next time was my brother, Jeremy.

Chapter Nine

I hate art class.

Because it is so noisy.

And because Aaron Miller is not in my art class, but Eric Doyle is. Eric Doyle doesn't look anything like Matthew Iverson from second grade. Not his hair, or his eyeglasses, or his voice—because Eric Doyle can't make an *R* sound—but for some reason I keep mixing the two of them up in my mind.

I also hate art class because I do not like Mrs. Hawthorne very much, because Mrs. Hawthorne does not like me. She started to not like me last week when I broke her potter's wheel. But I don't know if she liked me very much before that happened.

I didn't break her potter's wheel on purpose, but that doesn't mean it was an accident, because I was angry when it happened. If I hadn't been angry at Mrs. Hawthorne, I probably wouldn't have pushed the potter's wheel by accident. I wanted to push

Mrs. Hawthorne, but I knew I couldn't do that. I was controlling myself like my one-on-one aide, Jane, always told me, but Jane wasn't with me anymore. And besides, I didn't know the potter's wheel would fall over.

"Why did you do that?" Mrs. Hawthorne said.

"Because I am angry at you," I told her.

The potter's wheel was attached to a chair, and you were supposed to sit in the chair and put your allotment of wet clay on the wheel, and then the teacher would push the power button and the wheel would spin around. There are some potter's wheels that you have to spin with your own foot, but this one was electric.

Now it was in three pieces—the chair, the wheel that was still spinning, slowly, and the rest of the metal frame. There was also wet clay all over the floor of the art room and everyone was standing around looking.

I don't think Mrs. Hawthorne was even that mad. I could hear her voice was loud, but her body was still. And I knew I wasn't supposed to break things. If this meant I would have to have a one-on-one aide again, it would make my mother very sad.

I was sorry.

When I had broken things at home: the stained-glass hanging by the front door, the wicker laundry basket, the picture frame, the controller for my video game. When nobody could hear me. Nobody could understand. When there were no words in my head, then the thoughts built up inside me and had nowhere to go.

What had made me so angry with Mrs. Hawthorne in the first place? I couldn't remember anymore.

The energy that left my body and spilled into something else had finally ended and stopped and broke. The noise shattered my ears like a very tight band that was taken off my brain, and it was over.

But it's never really over.

Things stopped for a while. Everybody stopped, and it was quiet. Everybody was just looking at the mess.

There was the clay on the floor, landed in the shape of a dog, a sleeping dog. A big sleeping dog.

What sound does a dog make?

Did I really make a barking sound?

I don't remember, but suddenly everyone started laughing, like an explosion in the room. All around me, and *that* was when Mrs. Hawthorne got mad.

Or sad.

I was sorry. I was really sorry, but everyone was laughing. Their faces stretched out wide. I could see their teeth, and I started laughing too. Nothing felt funny, but I was laughing.

Then Mrs. Hawthorne ran out of the room, and when she was gone, some of the boys threw the clay around the room. I hid behind my hands, but I could hear their voices. One piece landed on her computer. The plastic keys made a hollow sound. Another plop of it hit Marcie Ford and got stuck in her hair. She started crying.

Later some of the parents wanted me out of the classroom. Nobody told me, but I knew it. The school called us all in for a

meeting. I knew my parents went in to the school to talk to
Dr. T.

I knew they were in battle mode.

This has nothing to do with having a one-on-one aide, my mother
was saying. *If another boy had accidentally knocked over a piece of
equipment, we wouldn't be having this meeting. And if the teacher
had done her job,* my father was saying. But I could have told him
it was no use, they couldn't hear his language either that day.

My dad just wasn't used to that like I am. So he kept trying
to talk.

All the grown-ups assumed I threw the clay, and none of the kids
ever said any different, but I don't think anyone asked them.

Certainly nobody asked me. Even right then at that meeting
with my parents.

Later Lara Mok told me her mother said I was dangerous and
shouldn't be in school with the normal kids. That I was disruptive
and holding everyone back. That it was only going to get worse.

She didn't mean for me.

For the NTs, she meant.

For the ones that threw the clay around the room and let me
take the blame.

All week Eric Doyle has made barking noises at me when I come
into the art room and sit down at my seat.

I am used to it.

Mrs. Hawthorne is trying to be nicer to me.

But I still don't like art class.

Mrs. Hawthorne shows us how to draw a face, with big eyes, black pupils, a capital letter *L* for the nose, and a half circle for the mouth all inside an oval circle that doesn't connect. Mrs. Hawthorne has to draw mine for me. She also helps the girl at the far left table, too, who broke her arm at a gymnastics meet.

Then, when everyone has as close to exactly the same thing on our paper, we are allowed to decorate the face with color. The girls put on eyelashes and red lips. The boys blacken the teeth and put on baseball caps. We do this project a few times every year. At Christmastime we can make the face into an elf or a Santa. For Halloween it can turn into a witch or a cat. It is a leprechaun if we color it green and Mrs. Hawthorne makes the ears like triangles.

I am staring at the lines on the paper. I don't see a face at all. I see straight black lines and white space. I see the distance from the top of the page to the arc and from the parallel lines to the end of my paper.

I see circles and half circles and the place where they intersect. I see the place where Mrs. Hawthorne lifted her marker and didn't connect the two lines. There are white spots like bubbles on the surface of the bathtub.

But nothing that looks like a face.

Nothing like the shadows, and pores, the hairs, the curves,

57

all the spots and wrinkles and blotches, the follicles, the wetness of the eye, saliva, teeth when it is laughing, all the planes and dimensions of a face.

And they say I can't recognize a face.

But Mrs. Hawthorne is going to be mad again if I don't start drawing.

"What are you doing, Jason?"

Mrs. Hawthorne's voice is like sand, like her words are being rubbed over sand. It hurts my ears to hear her voice. There is not a nice person behind that voice. I know I am right about that.

"Jason, you're not even trying."

So I put my hands over my ears, even though I know I am not supposed to do that.

My mom and dad fought really hard so that I could stay in class like everybody else, but I miss Jane. Jane would have known what to do.

She would have colored in my picture for me, or she would have said something to Mrs. Hawthorne so her sandy voice wouldn't burn my ears. She would take my hands down from my ears or my eyes and hold them in a way that wouldn't make me mad. She was round and soft and smelled like Dove soap and cookies.

But I don't need a one-on-one aide anymore.

That's what my mother says. That's what it says in my IEP,

which is more letters. More initials that define who I am.

I'll be on my own one day, my mother says. I need to start learning how to take care of myself.

But what I need now is to get Mrs. Hawthorne away from me.

Now I am sitting in the main office waiting for my dad to come and pick me up from school. That is also what it says in my IEP—that I get to go home from school whenever I feel like I can't handle it anymore. Or one of my teachers thinks that.

But this time I am sure it was me who thought it.

Usually my head would be ticking. I couldn't be breathing very well. The doors opening and closing down the hall echo, because the walls are all glass in here. The phone rings a funny ring. There is a two-way radio. The janitor must be walking by.

Usually I would hide behind my hands.

I know I should feel bad that I am going home from school, but all I can think of is one thing.

I am thinking that when I get home, I can check my website and maybe PhoenixBird has written to me again, and maybe I have one real friend. And that's all anyone needs, one.

One.

Plus one.

Makes two.

And then I am not as scared.

The word that popped into my brain this morning was "regurgitate."

Regurgitate.

But I can't think of how that relates to anything right now.

Chapter Ten

I write pretty much all of my stories using a first-person narrator so that the reader can really get an idea of what is going on inside my character's head. They can hear the story in that voice, and also so I can get inside my character's life.

And I can feel what he feels.

You have to decide if you want it to be in past or present tense. And the setting. You have to know where you want your story to take place.

When I get home, I see that PhoenixBird did send me the ending of her story. One day, she wrote, in the village a new baby is born who is different from all the other children before. As this child grows, she wants to help other people. No matter how many times people tell her they don't need her, she persists. She finds joy in helping people, "in the smallest ways. In the biggest ways."

Those are her words.

I like them.

"We're disappointed, Jason. That's all," my mother is saying.

"This hasn't happened all week, Jay-Jay. What happened?" my dad is saying.

Even though I thought I wanted to leave school, even though I got to check my website and write to PhoenixBird, everything felt out of place when I got home from school. It is not a holiday or vacation or a three-day weekend. It's a Friday, and I am having lunch at home. It is a Friday, and I am home but Jeremy is not. My dad is still here. He hasn't left for work yet.

My dad is never home when I get home from school.

All these things make my skin itch.

The sun doesn't look right coming into the kitchen.

I should not be here.

I should be in school.

I can feel my head, everything is in my head. My heart is beating inside my head. The sounds in my ears sound bigger and bigger. My breathing is tight coming in and out of my mouth.

I don't know what my body is doing anymore.

I don't want to let my parents down. I don't want my mother to say she is disappointed. But I couldn't think about that when Mrs. Hawthorne got too close to me.

I didn't push her or yell or do anything.

I could have wanted to, but I didn't.

I got under the table where I couldn't see her anymore, but she wouldn't stop her voice, and then the nurse had to come. And then I don't remember what happened exactly. Whose idea was it for me to come home from school?

I feel my father's arm all around me. I smell that cologne again, and the stubble of his face is rough, but I know it will not hurt me even though it feels like it could.

I let my dad hold me. He always leaves room for me to breathe. He never bends my back so I feel off balance. When my dad hugs me, I feel his feet holding us both up.

A narrator can be unreliable.

They can be telling the truth or just the truth as they see it. There is a famous book like that, where the narrator is lying. He judges everyone in the book except himself. And sometimes it's hard to tell what is really going on. Hard to tell what is real and what's not.

I didn't do anything to Mrs. Hawthorne to make her send me home.

But lots of people really think *The Catcher in the Rye* is a great book.

Before I go to bed tonight, I check the Storyboard website and see if anyone else posted anything about my story. And to check if PhoenixBird wrote me back again.

She did.

But her message doesn't have anything to do with her story or mine. She writes about her dog.

PhoenixBird has a dog named Blanche, who eats Cheerios and Chinese food, salad and even the tomatoes, but not the black olives and not the mushrooms. I would like to meet her dog one day, but I know that will never happen.

This is the kind of thing a friend would write to someone, to someone they wanted to have as a friend. I know I am right about this. I am pretty sure I am right.

`Today,` PhoenixBird wrote, `was Diversity Day at my school.`

She told me all about it, how great it was. I write her back, but I am not going to tell her about my day. Not about Mrs. Hawthorne. Not about hiding under the art table.

Something tells me that wouldn't be a good idea.

Chapter Eleven

Saturday we are going to visit our cousins in Glen Rock. It is my mother's brother, Uncle Bobby's house and his wife, Aunt Carol, and their two boys, Seth and Little Bobby. Whenever we visit there, my mom gets very nervous. If Grandma is going to be there too, my mother can't even find her pocketbook.

"Is everything in the car?"

"Yes, Liz," my dad tells her. "We're all set."

"My pocketbook," my mom is saying. "Where did I put my pocketbook?"

"It's on your shoulder." Jeremy laughs.

But Mom is not laughing. "Jeremy, your shirt. What did you get on your shirt? That was a clean shirt a minute ago. You haven't even eaten anything. Go change your shirt. Carl," she says to my dad, "go help Jeremy change his shirt. "

Then she turns to me, and I see her face change. The wrinkles all bunched up in her forehead smooth out. Her mouth drops, but she isn't frowning like she is mad or sad. If I hadn't seen this expression before, I would have no idea what it meant.

"Jason, your belt," my mother says, so softly. She has asked me this so many times. "Can you just loosen it a notch or two? Just for today?"

I can't.

I've tried, but it feels awful. I can feel the material of my pants sliding on my waist, moving and rubbing. I hate it. I know it looks funny. I know kids in school say things about my pants and my belt, how tight it is. How it bunches up in the back. One boy asked me if I was expecting a flood, and I had to ask Aaron Miller what that meant.

"Don't pay any attention to him, Jay-Man," Aaron told me, but I wanted to know, and I made him it explain it to me.

"Oh," I said. I looked down at my ankles and saw that my pants were pulled so tightly that my socks did show.

I like my shirt tucked in. I don't like how it feels when it's loose.

My mother takes one of the chairs from the dining room table and sits down so she is right next to where I am standing. I am standing, ready to go to Uncle Bobby's, waiting. I am waiting for everyone else to be ready.

"It's okay, Jason. I'm sorry." She doesn't pull me toward her, but she rests her head on my shoulder. "It's me. It's just me. I just can't stand hearing all about Seth anymore. And now, oh jeeze, Little Bobby. You'd think he'd won a Nobel Prize already."

My mother's hair smells like Herbal Essence and Curls Rock.

I remember when I was really little, when I was in nursery school, I refused to wear pants with zippers. I couldn't stand the feeling of the waistband and the stiffness of the material. My mother bought me leggings from this special catalog. They came in all different colors, and they were made of one hundred percent cotton. And she never made me wear pants.

I could run and lie down and nap in her arms when I was tired.

Then, when I got to kindergarten, one of the kids asked me if I was a ballet dancer.

"No," I said.

Then another boy asked me the same thing, even though he already knew, because he was there when I answered the first time.

This time I was more sure. "No," I said.

Then the last time one of the kids in my class asked me if I was a ballerina, my mother happened to be there listening.

And she took away all of my leggings.

"Isn't it funny, Jason?" my mother is saying. "Isn't it funny that when you were really little you wouldn't wear a belt at all? Isn't that funny?"

I love my mother so much.

"Remember, Jason?" she is saying. "Remember those leggings?"

We are both remembering the same thing.

"Those leggings?" I repeat what she has said, so she will know this.

"No?" my mother is saying. "You don't? It's okay. It was a long time ago. Well, let's go, shall we?"

Uncle Bobby is a big man as men go. He owns his own construction company. So even though he didn't go to school nearly as long as my dad, he makes three times as much money.

Yeah, and his wife has had more work done than any one of Uncle Bobby's biggest clients.

"But don't ever repeat that," my mother tells us in the car.

I don't even know what she means.

Aunt Carol has food out when we get there, big bowls and little bowls. Uncle Bobby asks everyone what they want to drink, except me.

"What can I get Jason?" Uncle Bobby asks my father.

"You can ask him yourself, Bob," my dad answers.

"How about a Coke then, son?" I can watch Uncle Bobby's

68

big feet and his big shoes head off into the kitchen.

My mother said I could bring my PlayStation Portable, and she lets me take it out. I also have a book. Jeremy and Little Bobby like to play with action figures, so that's what they are doing.

"You better run, Batman," my brother is saying. He is bouncing his little toy up and down in his hand.

"No, never, Mr. Freeze. This will be the end of you once and for all." Little Bobby is also bouncing his action figure. They bang the two toys into each other and make noises.

This makes Jeremy happy, and I don't understand at all what he is doing, because those little plastic figures don't look anything like the real superheroes, not in the cartoons or the movie versions, but I am happy for him.

"Seth, why don't you show Jason your new computer?" Aunt Carol says.

Seth has been sitting on the couch in the living room the whole time, eating from the different bowls of food. Aunt Carol has been telling us all about Seth, even though he is sitting right there. I hear that Seth is on the math team and that he volunteers to tutor kids in the elementary school on Tuesdays and Wednesdays. I hear that Seth is in advanced language arts and that he made the travel soccer team.

My mother looks over to me from time to time and tries to

catch my eye, and then she arches her back and lifts her chin way up in the air. This is her way of telling me to sit up straight.

I sit up and I forget and then back down.

My mother looks tired of doing this.

Seth has also been asked to model for a local department store.

"Oh, Seth. A new computer. Jason loves computers. Don't you, Jason?" my mother says. "He's so good at computers. I don't know a thing."

The word that came into my head this morning while we were getting ready to visit our cousins was halogen. That's what I try to think about now.

"I can't even turn the darn thing on by myself." My mother's laugh doesn't sound right. "Jason has to help me with everything, don't you?"

"So why don't you show your cousin your new computer, Seth?" Aunt Carol says. "And Aunt Liz and I can get dinner ready."

This is what I notice:

NTs will lie.

And it's not that I can't.

I could.

If I wanted to.

But even when everyone who is listening knows it's a lie, they can pretend it's not, and then everybody is lying. The listeners and the tellers.

And it's hard for me to tell what is real and what is not.

Seth tells his mother his computer isn't working.

He says the hard drive needs to be rebooted and he has to call technical assistance because there is some special override code.

And he says he'd be happy to do all that, but that once he starts the process he can't stop, and it might take an hour or more. He says he doesn't want it to interfere with dinner. And Aunt Carol and my mother both say they don't want that to happen.

Then we get into Seth's room, because his mother makes him take me anyway, he sits right down at his computer, which seems to be working just fine, and starts playing Halo.

"Don't touch anything," he tells me.

I can look at his back while he sits in his chair. I can hear the banging of his fingers on the keyboard. I already knew I wouldn't get to check my website until I got home tonight, but I am not upset about that.

I sit down on the rug in the middle of the room.

I can see the green leaves of a tree outside Seth's bedroom

window that move with the wind, and even though I can't hear it, it makes a kind of music. A silent dance, swaying in a rhythm I know is there. All over the tree, branches lift and drop, and the light falls from one leaf to the one below, and one tiny shadow on the bark is like the youngest child, walking behind his family, lost in his own world and perfectly content.

"What's wrong with you, man?" Seth has spun around in his chair. "Your brother is talking to you," Seth is telling me.

Jeremy puts his hand on my face, small and warm and sweaty. He came into the dark room when the sun moved behind a cloud, and now the only light is the glow from Seth's computer. I can hear the chimes of his IMs, sending and receiving. Tiny bells.

"Jason?" Jeremy is saying. When I look away from the window, he takes his hand from my face. "Can you reach something for us? For me and Bobby."

His breath smells like Starbursts.

"What are you asking him for?" Seth is saying.

Jeremy always asks me to do things for him. He asks me to zip his jacket. He asks me to check his spelling. To carry things that are too heavy for him. To push him on the swings. Before he agrees to taste something he's never eaten before, Jeremy asks me if he'll like it.

"Can you, Jason?" Jeremy says to me again.

He must want me to reach something that is too high for him to reach. Of course I will.

"If it's up that high, you're not supposed to have it. Did you ever think of that?" Seth says. I know he is talking to me and

Jeremy, but I can't look up. I don't know what I will see. There is his voice and his presence in the room, and the darkness of the sun behind the clouds, the chiming of his computer. There is the creaking of his chair, and the scent of his clothing as he walks toward us. It all sounds too loud and too angry.

Even the fan whirling on the ceiling of the room is yelling at me in a mechanical voice that has no words. Seth should just stop.

Being.

This is when you are supposed to leave a situation.

Walk away.

Breathe.

"Yeah, good. Why don't you and your defective brother get out of my room already," Seth says. "You're smelling the place up."

The rest happens very fast.

Then Seth is yelling and then he falls over his swivel chair. The swivel chair spins out from under Seth's weight and careens into his stack of CDs, which then tumble onto the rug. Then there is the cracking, crackling noise of CD covers being stepped on and snapping into two. Or maybe three.

Or more.

Jeremy's hand, I know it's Jeremy's, pulling me.

And then outside Seth's bedroom door there is air again.

"Good shot, Jason," my brother is saying to me.

He is happy, but I know our parents will not be, for some reason.

"Don't worry, I won't tell you kicked Seth," Jeremy says to me.

I look up quickly at Jeremy's face. It is bursting with a smile, and then it is bursting with laughter. Me too.

I see the light coming in the skylight above the hall, freed from behind the clouds, and the laughter. I feel them both, in my head and my hands and my eyes.

Chapter Twelve

This night I am writing a new story to post on Storyboard. The whole idea came to me on the car ride home from Uncle Bobby's. It is about a dwarf—not a midget, because dwarfs do not like to be called midgets, even though there was a time when "dwarf" was the bad word and "midget" was better.

But now it's the complete opposite.

Titles. Names. More words, the same twenty-six letters strung together that sometimes hurt someone and sometimes don't.

My dwarf in my story is named Bennu. He is one of those disproportional dwarfs, so his arms and legs are very short in proportion to his body, and it makes his head look big. But basically he is pretty comfortable with his height and his looks, and lots of other normal people of normal height like him. But being a dwarf is a handicap. He is not just different, but defective.

He has his family, who are all normal height. That is the way it happens. He could even have normal-sized kids, if he got a girlfriend and then got married. If that ever happened.

I put Bennu in a made-up world, so I got to make up all the names and all the different kinds of people who live there. Life is definitely harder for Bennu, not only because people stare at him and sometimes laugh when he goes out (which is bad enough), but for other real reasons. Like he can't reach things other people his age can, like door handles or the top shelf of the fridge where the milk is.

There are many doors he can't open by himself.

And some things about his genetic condition are painful. His back hurts because his spine is compressed, and his legs sometimes ache.

Sometimes just being Bennu is very hard to be.

Names are very important when writing a story.

I think a long time when I am giving a character a name. I have to know everything about them before I know what they will be called. You have to take several things into consideration when you give a character a name. Who they are, where they are from, in what time period your story is set. And sometimes names can have symbolic meanings, like in the famous book *To Kill a Mockingbird*. I haven't read it yet, but you can search online and learn everything about famous books. I guess you could even pretend you have read a book and pretty much get away with it just by reading one of those websites.

Some people, like teachers and librarians and other adults, like to say that names are not important.

Like sticks and stones.

But they are wrong.

Every word you choose means something you think it means, and more.

Like if a person is *different*, that is a good thing.

But if they have a *defect*, that is not.

Words.

Names.

Letters.

I post this first installment of my story at 9:13 p.m.

I think, it's late, but I am wondering if PhoenixBird will read it tonight.

And I wonder if she will notice. Will she figure it out?

I wonder if she will get it.

Bennu is the Egyptian name for the mythical bird who rose from its own ashes. A bird whose song was so beautiful that everyone who heard it had to stop to listen and whose tears were known to heal the wounded. Bennu is the Egyptian word for phoenix. For phoenix bird.

Chapter Thirteen

My dad comes into my room to tell me to turn off my computer and get ready for bed.

It's easier to be around my dad, because he talks less. That doesn't mean I don't love my mom, but a lot of the time she makes me feel like she wants something from me. It pulls me, like a drain draining water after a bath, that sucking noise it makes at the very end. Not many people wait around long enough to hear that sound, but I do.

Anyway, I know my dad wants to talk to me about what happened at Uncle Bobby's. He's waited all evening to talk to me.

But I knew it was coming. For a long while my dad doesn't say anything. He just looks up at our ceiling.

"Are things okay, Jason?" he asks me. He keeps his eyes away from me.

I nod. I know he can see me from the side.

"Is there anything bothering you that you want to talk about?" he asks.

A couple of years ago I figured out that my dad's arms around me don't really make the darkness, the anger, the sadness go away. They just postpone it for a while. This doesn't stop me, though, from wondering what my dad can help me with and what he can't. And what will happen when he's not around anymore.

Who will take care of me?

My dad is sitting at the end of my bed.

"It's okay to be sad, Jason. It's okay to be afraid," my dad is saying. "It's even okay to be angry, Jason."

I want to believe him.

"It's not okay to hurt someone else."

Now it's hard to breathe.

"Calm down, Jason. And don't pull your hair," my father says. He takes my hands and puts them at my sides. My hands are feeling like flying. My hair is itching, maybe burning. Maybe this is what it feels like to be on fire.

"Jason." My father's voice is louder, stronger. "You're not in trouble and I am not mad at you."

Mad.

Sad.

Dad.

That is a word family. Like cat, hat, bat.

I'm sorry, Daddy. I'm sorry you are so sad about me.

80

All you have to do is change one letter, and the whole word is different. Like people. I wish I could change one letter and make everything better.

But I can't, Daddy.

After I kicked Seth, and he fell, and then somebody stepped on a lot of his CDs, Aunt Carol came running up the stairs. My mother was right behind her. Seth was yelling so much, so loud. The cracking of the CD covers. The thumping of the footsteps on the stairs. Heels clicking on the wooden floor, coming closer. Harsh snapping of hard plastic.

"Jason, what did you do? Jason!" Aunt Carol started shouting.

"What happened?" my mother said, but she wasn't really asking that.

And Jeremy got really mad. He was saying things, fast words. Talking about me, his brother, how I needed to help him, about Seth, about reaching something in Little Bobby's closet. I could hear his fear, and his anger.

"We *were* allowed to have it," Jeremy was saying. He said it again.

It was all too much. Seth was moaning and holding his leg. His mother was screaming for Uncle Bobby to get some ice.

"For God's sake, Bobby, hurry. Ice."

When Uncle Bobby, my mother, Aunt Carol, Seth still on the

floor, Jeremy, Little Bobby, and then my dad were all in the room, I felt the ceiling explode over my head. It was my head. My head exploded.

There was no way to stop all the molecules that started penetrating my skin.

My hands flew off my body.

My body flew into a million little pieces.

I could smell the fresh coffee that Aunt Carol and my mother had put up for dessert as we hurried out the front door. I could smell the pastries she would have put out, and I wanted one.

Chapter Fourteen

I tell Aaron Miller I have a girlfriend.

"Hey, that's great," he says to me.

We are in the cafeteria: loud voices, bright lights, strong food smells, *and* garbage. Jane used to sit with me every day. Now I have to find someone on my own. I am grateful I see Aaron sometimes.

I sat down with Aaron and the two other boys he is sitting with.

"What's her name?" he asks.

And this is when I realize I probably shouldn't have said anything.

Because I don't know her name, not her real name.

But one of the other boys at the table starts talking about something else. He is talking about the game last night, and that's good. Besides, my mother wants me to buy lunch this year, so I have a tray in front of me, and now I have to figure out what everything is and what I can eat.

There are only eighteen minutes left of lunch period. I have to concentrate.

I barely finish, but I was lucky, because today was meat loaf, mashed potatoes and gravy, chilled peaches, dinner rolls, and ice cream cups, and I could eat it all.

"Well, Jay-Man, guess you were hungry," Aaron is saying to me. He is getting up from the table, scrunching his paper bag into a wrinkly brown ball. I know he will throw it into the trash can from here.

He does.

"So maybe someday we will get to meet this girl, huh?" he says to me. He rubs the top of my head, and he is gone.

Meet this girl?

That could never happen.

I don't even know her name.

The rest of the day is without incident.

Although it bothers me.

Because up until that moment it hadn't bothered me at all.

And now it does all the rest of the day.

What is PhoenixBird's name?

Then I start to imagine what she looks like, and that she must have hair and a face, hands and legs and feet with shoes. Well, I can't really imagine what she looks like, but I have the thought that she must look like something that has a face and hair, maybe long.

And girl shoes.

A girl's face. A girl's voice.

"What are you doing, Jason?"

And before you know it, I have torn the first page of my math workbook into many, many small pieces that lie on the floor by my desk. When I look down, I see them. It looks like snow, and I know we learned that no two snowflakes are alike. Of the billions and hundreds of billions, no two are exactly the same. The staggering number of possibilities within the hundreds of configurations of each water molecule of vapor as it turns into a hexagonal form of ice. And even though it looks flat, it's not. It is an amazingly complex structure, an amazingly beautiful thing. So even though teachers make you fold paper and cut out little triangles, spread it out and tape it to the window, snow is not really flat. It is not that simple.

"Jason, this is unacceptable behavior."

That is my math teacher talking, and I have forgotten her name. She looks so much like the nurse at my pediatrician's office. They both have very short red hair, and I can't tell them apart. So I don't try.

The kids are starting to laugh again, which doesn't bother me, but I know it will make the teacher very nervous. Teachers don't like it when kids are laughing, unless it is because they have made a joke they think is funny, and then they get upset if the kids don't laugh.

"I'm sorry, Jason, but you are going to have to stay and clean this up while the rest of the class goes across the hall to watch Mrs. Santoro's class's geometry play."

It is a good thing for me that I don't want to see that play at all.

I don't mind picking up all the little pieces of paper, and now it is quiet in the classroom. Only the math teacher sitting at her desk writing.

She thinks she is holding me responsible for my actions.

I am on the floor under my desk.

The pieces of paper don't look anything like snowflakes anymore. I can see the jagged, frayed edges of white where I tore it and tore it.

I start to think of how many times in one day does something like this happen to me. And how I am so used to not getting what I want. How many times I am on the floor under my desk picking up pieces of paper, metaphorically speaking, that is.

Every day, maybe twenty times a day. Maybe more.

So PhoenixBird is my girlfriend.

Inside my computer.

I just need to remember not to talk about her anymore.

So the *rest* of the day is without incident.

Chapter Fifteen

Jeremy wants the plate with the dividers at dinner tonight.

But our mom has taken them away.

She says he has to get used to eating off a regular plate, because not everybody in the world will be able to accommodate him, but again I know she is really talking about me. In code.

Jeremy starts to cry.

Right at the table.

Boys are not supposed to cry. I learned that about the same time I figured out that my mom and dad couldn't make everything all right, even when they say, *Don't worry. Everything is going to be all right.*

It's not.

Boys are not supposed to cry. Because when they do, things get worse. Then suddenly you have two problems. You have whatever it was that made you cry in the first place, and then you also have the problem that you are a boy crying. And someone is bound to let you know this is worse. So now you have two problems.

Better not to cry, Jeremy, I want to tell him.

"Jeremy, what's the matter?" my mother is saying.

At first people will always act like crying is okay.

"I want my plate. I want my plate with the little rooms in it." He is crying.

"But Jeremy, you can use this plate. It's fine. None of your food is touching. Look," she says. "And even if it does . . . it's fine."

And then, after that, they try to tell you why you shouldn't be crying.

"It's fine, Jeremy," my dad says.

"No, I can't eat. I want my plate." Tears are dropping off his face. His voice is clogged with wetness like mucus in his throat.

It is like the snowflakes that fall to the ground, each one different from every other one. But no one can see that. All they see is white and flat. And it all looks the same. And that is the way they like it.

The food is like that for Jeremy. He just doesn't know it yet.

"Sometime your food is going to have to touch," I tell my brother.

It gets really quiet at the table.

"What?" my mother asks me. "What did you say, Jason?"

I look down at my plate. The food is far enough apart, but it never bothered me. It was always Jeremy. Jeremy needed those plates. I don't understand why he shouldn't have one, but I know he can't. I see now that even Jeremy has to learn what I have known all my life.

You don't always get what you need.

So I say it again, even though I am sure my mother heard me.

"Sometime your food is going to have to touch. It's not so bad. You get used to it."

"There, see?" she says, but I have a feeling my mother has heard something else.

"Don't cry," my dad tells him. "C'mon, Jeremy. Eat some dinner. It's good."

"Don't cry, sweetie," my mother says. "Look, Jason lets his food touch."

Jeremy is still sniffling, but he picks up his fork.

Then, finally, you figure out it's better not to cry in the first place.

Chapter Sixteen

One day a very old and very wise scientist comes to the town where Bennu lives with his family. It is not by chance that this famous doctor has arrived. He is *looking* for Bennu, because the doctor believes he has found a cure for dwarfism. He has traveled many miles over treacherous land to find Bennu. He believes he has invented an operation that can make Bennu look pretty much like everyone else.

Also, the doctor believes that with his cure he can make sure no one will be born with the same problem ever again.

This installment ends just as the doctor delivers his message to Bennu and his family.

It's a good idea to leave your reader wanting more. It's called a cliffhanger, like your character is hanging by his fingertips on the edge of a very steep cliff. I upload my chapter on the Storyboard website, but the only reader I really care about anymore is PhoenixBird. Maybe she lives in a different time zone. Two hours later. Maybe she will read it before she goes to school. Or two hours earlier, and maybe she will have already left for school and she'll have read it before I get home. How can I find out what her real name is?

Then before I have to leave for school, I send her a little note, just to let her know my story is posted on the website.

And by the way, I write at the end of my message, my real name is Jason.

Very tricky, if I must say so myself.

Next to art class, physical education class is the worst. Most kids call it PE class. But I don't like those letters together that way.

Mostly it's because of the noise, the way the noise races around the gym, hits the high ceiling, where it all gathers together between the metal light shades and gets louder before falling back down again.

"So you have a girlfriend, Jason?"

It is the boy from Aaron's table, one of the boys who eat lunch with him sometimes. I ate lunch with them last week. I shouldn't have.

The boy is laughing, but I know this kind of laugh.

"And you don't even know her name," the boy is saying. Laughing.

There are lines on the floor of the gym, blue lines and yellow and white and red. One line is the farthest outside of all the others, never intersecting, not bending, never touching the others. Parallel lines that continue into infinity and never meet.

The boy is talking to me but not talking to me. He is talking loudly, even though no one else is listening to him. His voice bounces off the blue cushioned walls.

"*I* know what her name is," he says.

He does?

Does he know her?

Does this boy know PhoenixBird?

I will not be able to breathe.

He is laughing more. Louder.

"You wanna know what her name is?" he is saying.

If he knows PhoenixBird, she will have told him the truth. He will know she is not really my girlfriend. My hair hurts. My chest is tight.

"I bet her name is Retardo Girl," the boy says.

No, I am thinking. *Her name can't be Retardo Girl.*

Can it?

"And I bet she rides the little bus to school."

And then I figure it out. He is just being mean. When a dog gets mean and bites a person, it's the law that they have to put that dog to sleep. This boy is just being mean. He is lying. He doesn't really know PhoenixBird. I have nothing to worry about. For some reason my head is still shaking.

But I can breathe.

Mr. DeMateo comes out and starts throwing basketballs onto the floor. They all bounce up and down at different times, like drummers who can't hear each other, and then roll until someone picks one up and shoots it at the hoop.

And misses.

"Lexicon" is the word that came to me this morning.

Even before I got out of bed.

Chapter Seventeen

Last year, I was eleven years old and Jeremy was just eight, our dog, Lester, got very sick, and we had to put him to sleep.

Which is another one of those expressions when someone doesn't want to say what they really mean.

We had gotten Lester from the Humane Society in the next town over. I was four when I went with my mom to pick him out, but of course we didn't know he would be a *him* when we went.

They don't let you put a dog "on hold." You can go back as many times as you want and look till you find the dog you want, but once you see one, you have to decide right then and there.

I was the one that wanted a dog.

And getting Lester was a reward, but I don't remember anymore for what.

I wanted a dog so badly.

So badly I let my mother lead me into the dark, wet, concrete hallway where they kept the dogs, even though the smell was so bad it burned my eyes and my tongue. Every single dog was barking, all at once, jumping up and putting their paws on the fronts of their cages. Jumping up and then running back, spinning around and then pouncing on the bars again as we passed.

There were plastic bags hanging from each cage with a piece of white paper inside. My mother listened as I read the names out loud, because I could read every word.

"That's amazing," the Humane Lady said as we made our way down the long, wet, concrete hall. "How old is he?"

"Four," my mother said. "He's only just four."

Lester was the only dog that wasn't barking. He wasn't even jumping up on his cage. He was sitting straight up, looking right out at us, trembling, trembling. He was shaking so hard you could see the motion from the top of his head, back and forth to the end of his body.

He was so scared.

"Beagle mix," I read. "Eleven months old. Lester."

I really didn't talk much in those days, and I knew I wanted Lester, but what would happen to the other dogs if we didn't pick them? I hated it in that place. It was cold and dark, that horrible smell and that horrible loneliness. I stopped walking and stood in front of Lester's cage. My mother stopped too, and so did the Humane Lady.

Lester shook even harder.

"This one?" the lady asked me.

But I was sad, so sad. Too sad. The other dogs were barking and standing up to be picked, to be taken out of this place. I wanted to say something. I wanted to ask, but I couldn't find the words. I opened my mouth, but nothing came out.

"Every dog here finds a home," the lady said. "We have a hundred percent adoption rate."

Lester. We took Lester home with us that day. He pooped and peed and threw up in our car, which made me cry and scream, too, but we both got home. My mother asked me if I wanted to give him a new name, but I didn't.

You can't change what you are called. Good or bad, it's your name.

That night I wrote down all the names and breeds of every dog we saw, and Lester slept at the end of my bed.

And then Lester got sick.

So sick the doctor told us there was nothing he could do.

Lester was only seven years old, and even in dog years that is pretty young.

My dad tried to tell me and Jeremy at dinner one night that they were going to have to put Lester to sleep, to die.

"The vet did everything he medically could," our dad said.

"We gave Lester a very good life," my mother said.

Jeremy was crying so hard his snot was running down his face. I was just listening.

"Lester is very sick," my mother said. "That's how nature works sometimes. There is nothing we can do."

I knew my parents were telling the truth. We had taken Lester to the doctor every week for months, and he had ten bottles of medicine on the kitchen counter.

"We have taken very good care of him. He's had a good, good life," our dad said. "You know, you have to remember Lester is a dog. And imagine, if Lester lived in the wild, he wouldn't have lasted this long."

But Lester didn't live in the wild.

He lived with us.

Rebecca.

Her name is Rebecca.

That's definitely a girl's name.

There was a message from PhoenixBird when I got home from school. She had read my story. And my note.

And she told me her real name.

Rebecca.

I really care about Bennu, she wrote. Your story is great. I felt like I could feel what he was feeling

anything but typical

and thinking. Like I could really see and hear him. And there is so much symbolism in your story. How do you do that? Do you outline? Do you know what is going to happen in the end?

There is a PS at the end of her message, which stands for postscript, meaning something you thought about after you've finished your whole letter, so you have to add it to the end.

PS. you'll never believe it.

Today after school Blanche found the lunch I didn't eat. She ate a hole right through my backpack to get to it. Then she got sick on our living room carpet. I don't which my mom is more mad about, the rug or my new knapsack. LOL.

That's the kind of stuff friends tell each other.

And her name is Rebecca.

I am thinking of what to write back to Rebecca, my friend.

Who is a girl.

Chapter Eighteen

At first Bennu's family seems overjoyed by the news the famous doctor brings to town. Right to their doorstep, in fact. Bennu stands back and listens. Of course, everything occurs a few feet over his head, because he is so short. But in a way this is an advantage for Bennu. He has learned to listen better.

He hears what the doctor proposes.

Your son won't be short anymore, the doctor tells everyone.

But we don't want everyone to be the same, do we? Bennu's father says.

No, but if you agree to the operation, the doctor promises, *no one will look at Bennu ever again and know anything is wrong.*

No, Rebecca, I write back, I don't know how my story is going to end. I don't even know what Bennu and his family are going to decide yet. That's usually where I get all messed up. I try and let my characters tell me what they want to have happen.

We are on an E schedule this week. So it's library day again, and I get to check my Storyboard site, but then it turns out we aren't having library. There are teacher meetings in the library and we can't go in there. I have to wait until I get home, except I have an appointment with my talk therapist and I don't get home until dinner. My talk therapist is different from my OT, my occupational therapist, because mostly with my TT we just sit there and do nothing. Sometimes she tries to get me to talk by showing me pictures. Lots of neurotypical people go to talk therapists too. Lots of NTs go to TTs.

Even my mom does.

My talk therapist told my mom I am being very patient and I am learning to delay gratification. I get a Hershey's Kiss as a reward when I leave the office, which I give to Jeremy because I don't like chocolate.

My brain is about to burst from so much gratification delaying, by the time I get up to my room and boot up my computer. My skin hurts from waiting. My flying hands try to soothe my skin. My feet are tapping because my hands are flying, which makes my skin hurt more. And finally I can read my message from Rebecca.

You must be really good in language arts, she writes.

Then she tells me all about her day.

PS, she writes again. So sorry to hear about your dog, Lester. He sounds like he was really special and he was lucky to have you.

I have never felt lucky before, that I can remember.

But I do now.

My parents are happy with me.

I haven't had to leave school for any reason in over a month.

All my teachers gave me good progress reports, even my art teacher, Mrs. Hawthorne. And the probation period for not having a one-on-one aide has passed. We have another IEP, and it is decided I should stay inclusionary. No one-on-one necessary at this point in time.

They think now is a good time to tell me about a trip they have planned for me. They were going to wait to tell me, but they think it's a good time right now.

Kind of a reward, they tell me.

They are big on rewards. My mom and dad have come into my room at the same time. They never do that. There is barely enough room.

"Would you like to go to the Storyboard convention this year?" my mom is asking me.

There are Storyboard conventions every year, all over the United States and hundreds of people go to them. Some people go dressed in costumes of their favorite characters, with fake ears, hats with horns, swords, and lightsabers, and most of the stories are either from movies or books that were made into movies. And then you notice that sometimes they even start using the *actors'* names in their stories instead of the characters'.

That's just plain confusing.

The Storyboard convention is for all the people who post on the different Storyboard websites. All the different ages. Lots of people go. It's something I've been talking about ever since I found the website.

"Yes, we mean it," my mom says.

She must be reacting to my face, because I didn't say anything.

"We know how much it means to you and how long you've wanted to go," my dad says. "We'd like all four of us to go, but that would be a little bit too expensive, so just you and one of us. Either Mom or me."

Either Mom or Dad?

Mom hands me a brochure for the Storyboard Sixth Annual Writing Conference in Dallas, Texas.

"It's not just that fan fiction stuff," she tells me.

"There are writing workshops," my dad says. "On all different topics."

"And readings," my mom says. "From published authors. Real writers."

"Like you're going to be one day," my dad says.

I put my head on his shoulder, and I let my eyes close. I put my hand on my mother's leg, and she puts her hand on top of mine.

I am going to Dallas, Texas.

Truthfully, language arts *is* my best class, but not because I have a good grade in it. I like it because there are no right answers, even if the teacher says there are. Even when they mark something wrong on your test or book report, it's really just their opinion, and in my opinion they could be wrong. It's like when you read the directions on the back of a package of brownie mix.

Two eggs or three?

Do you want chewy or cakelike?

There is no wrong answer.

Books are like brownies.

I also like language arts because everyone asks me for help.

"Jason, can you fill in this last page in my vocabulary book?" Kids who don't ever talk to me otherwise. "But make the handwriting messier so it looks like mine."

"Jason, how do you spell 'definitely'?"

"'Veterinarian'?"

"'Facetious'?"

"Hey, what happens at the end of this book, Jason? It was so boring I couldn't finish it."

"How about 'potato'? Is there an E at the end?"

When I ask my language arts teacher for my homework for next Friday, because I am going to miss school, because me and my dad are leaving for Texas. He asks me where I am going.

"Texas."

Mr. Shupack laughs, the nice laughing. "I know, Jason. But where? What are you going there for? Do you have family there? Do you have family in Texas?"

Mr. Shupack is pretty nice. He is very tall and has facial hair that connects from his sideburns all the way around to his chin and under his nose. There is no mistaking him for someone else. I always feel comfortable around him, even when he thinks he's right all the time, but I hate looking at the birthmark on his arm. I try never to see it.

I look at him out of the corner of my eye.

"No," I say. "I am going to the Storyboard writing convention in Dallas, Texas."

I think he will like this, since he is an English teacher and they are supposed to like writing. And then I realize I am not leaving for another week and a half, and maybe Mr. Shupack doesn't know what the homework will be that far in advance. I remember that I have not yet told my parents which one of them I want to come with me. And my dad says he needs to know so he can make the reservations. He told me that this morning when I was brushing my teeth.

So then I say, "Vizcaíno."

It is the word that came into my head this morning, but I didn't think of it until just now. I was thinking of too many things when it first came to me. And now it comes to me again.

It always just happens like that.

"The pitcher?" Mr. Shupack says.

"What?"

But now I know I shouldn't have said it out loud. It was the consonant sounds, the slippery, sliding sound of the word. Remembering this morning and the decision I have to make.

"Luis Vizcaíno? The guy who used to pitch for the New York Yankees?" Mr. Shupack says.

I had no idea. Sometimes that happens.

I must have heard it somewhere.

On TV maybe.

"No," I say. "My father."

I am sure now.

Chapter Nineteen

The most important thing to do when you are writing a story is to find a dilemma for your character to grapple with. You can have the greatest, most interesting characters, and you can have something really important you want to say, but you need a story. You need conflict.

And you don't have to look very far. It's all been written before.

In every book in the library.

Every fable and myth, every play and legend, every fairy tale and story.

You can make up this whole new world and all these amazing characters, but it's just that in order to make a story, basically, something bad has to happen.

It's not that I don't know that my mother is upset, or that I don't know why. I just don't know what I could do about it.

"Your mother gets her feelings hurt easily," my dad tells me. "But she understands."

I don't.

Because I don't talk much, my mother thinks I am not feeling. For my mother, *talking* about feelings and *feeling* feelings are the same thing. But for me they're not.

So she is sitting very quietly, watching TV, and she looks okay, but I know she's not.

My dad is on the phone making airline reservations. I know my mother wanted me to pick her, even though she didn't really want to go. My mother doesn't like to travel. She doesn't like to leave the house, really. She gets nervous when she has to drive to new places. She always turns right when the directions say left, and then she looks like she is about to cry. She gets lost pretty much every time she goes somewhere she has never been before. So she tries not to do that.

Which makes perfect sense to me.

Why do something that you're not very good at? Why?

"Women like to know they are wanted," my dad told me. "They want to know they are needed."

I want to—

Sit right next to my mother.

On the couch and touch her. Touch her hair. I used to love the feel of the smoothness between my fingers, and when I was little, I wouldn't even realize I was touching her hair, in and out, between my first two fingers. I could see the color with the touch of my hands. I could hear the rhythm when I closed my eyes, like water over slippery rocks.

Touching my mother's hair was soothing, and that's why I did it. So now I am too old for the soothing, but I never seem too old to have the stress.

I have a lot of stresses.

If I had asked my mother to take me to Dallas, Texas, would my father be upset instead? Maybe, but he wouldn't be sitting in his quiet, like my mother is. And what about Jeremy—maybe he's mad because nobody ever takes him anywhere?

Except Jeremy did go to Six Flags Great Adventure. Twice.

I really want to go to the convention. I want to be around all those people who write stories and talk about stories. Around real writers whose characters come to life in their minds so real they can hardly tell what they are trying to say from what their character is actually saying.

I want to e-mail Rebecca and tell her my good news.

Maybe I *am* lucky.

I am thinking Rebecca will be very excited for me that I am going to the convention, like Mr. Shupack was.

And maybe someday *I* will be a famous writer.

Maybe someday I will write a book about my life.

I can see Bennu, in my mind, considering all his options. I am seeing him looking at the other people around him, but I know I have to put him somewhere to do this. Like at a party or in school. So he can see lots of different people and think about whether he wants to be more like they are.

I have to think really hard what it would feel like to be so short. What the world would look like to him. What he would look like to the world. And what can I have happen that will make things any worse than they already are for Bennu?

And then I have to listen.

I have to listen and let Bennu tell me what he wants to say.

I can't wait to tell Rebecca about my trip to the convention. I am sitting at my computer for a long while before I want to turn it on. I am thinking about how I will write to Rebecca.

So that she will be most impressed.

It is the upper right-hand corner button, and you have to hold it down for at least two seconds. You can't just push it like the other keys on the keyboard.

I like the noise my hard drive makes when it begins to wind up.

The whirling and grinding noises, like there are little gears inside cranking, little tiny lights blinking on. The fan starts spinning. The screen goes from black to dark blue. And besides, I like to give my computer a rest at night. Not to always be on alert, as if any moment it has to light up and start working. I like to give it a little warning.

All the icons appear on the screen, one by one.

And then it prompts me for my password.

I am still thinking of Bennu. In a way I can actually see him, but not the way you'd see a real person standing in front of you or in a movie even, but the way you see a memory. The way you see a dream. The way the words, and images, and realness and not real all get mixed up. The way you can remember a dream and know exactly what happened, and what that person who sold you the giant ice cream cone looked like, but it doesn't translate into being awake.

The letters are the same, but the language is different.

I am ready to write a message to Rebecca, but I see that she has already written to me, even though it was my turn next.

Jason, you'll never believe this. She writes, The Storyboard convention is going to be right in my hometown this year. And guess what . . . I am going to go! There are tons of workshops and some real authors

will be there. I will make sure to take really good
notes and I will share everything with you when I get
home. Yours truly, she writes. Rebecca.

I think something bad has just happened.

Chapter Twenty

My parents want to know what's wrong.

That is the question I hate second most in the world.

Is something wrong?

My mother is asking me, "Honey, is something wrong?"

"What's going on, Jason?" my father is asking me.

I can't answer this question. It would be like trying to catch drops of water at the bottom of a waterfall. That's just what it feels like, a ton of water falling on my head. Constantly bombarding my brain. It's hard to breathe under all this falling weight of water.

I can't let Rebecca really see me.

Pounding.

She'll know exactly who I am.

Falling.

Who am I?

I want to get a haircut now. My hair is killing me.

I can't go to the convention now. No, I can't tell you why. I can't tell anyone.

"Jason, stop pulling at your hair. Jason, stop. Stop flapping. Look at me. What's wrong?" My mother is saying.

Jeremy is quiet.

He is always quiet when I am loud.

And the other way around.

Everybody was somewhere else, but now they are all here. In the hallway. I have to throw something, from my hand, into space. Into the space that is attacking my brain. I have to throw the thing that I feel is in my hand.

But none of this probably would have happened if my mother hadn't come into my room in the first place. She opened the door to my room without knocking. Even my talk therapist has said she is supposed to knock.

"Are you all right?"

That is the question I hate first and the most.

"Jason, are you all right?"

Am I ever all right?

"Jason, I am talking to you," she went on.

Rebecca likes me. She thinks I'm a good writer.

"I heard noises up here," my mother said. She was still standing in my doorway.

She's my girlfriend.

But she won't be for long.

"Jason, stop it. You're going to hurt yourself."

But nothing could hurt more than this.

I am awake but dreaming. I can see Rebecca seeing me, even though I have never seen Rebecca and I don't know what she looks like. Now she is wearing a T-shirt with a picture of a great scarlet bird, two-dimensional, its head to the side, its wings spread like arms, surrounded by flames. That is how I know it is her.

It is crowded in the convention hall. And hot, because it is Texas. There are tables set up when you first walk in, two tables with big signs that say IF YOUR LAST NAME STARTS WITH A–L and another one that says, IF YOUR LAST NAME STARTS WITH M–Z. There are three people sitting at each table, and people are already pushing to get to the front and sign in. The check-in people are very friendly; I can tell by their voices. I am sure if I could look up they would be smiling. My dad does all the talking. When I start to rock a little, my dad doesn't even act like he notices. If he cares that the lady next to us on my left, is looking at me and that she even takes two very tiny steps away, he doesn't let on.

When you sign in, you get a name tag, which is not the sticky peel-off kind but a real one in a plastic sleeve that hangs on an elastic cord to put around your neck.

And my dad gets one too.

I look down at the tag hanging around my neck:

JASON BLAKE

WESTON, CONNECTICUT

STORYBOARD MEMBER

THREE YEARS

There is no escape now.

The thing that I threw at my mom to make her stop talking to me hit Jeremy instead.

Luckily, it was just my computer mouse.

But his head bled a lot.

It's easy to feel bad about yourself.

And then even worse.

Chapter Twenty-one

It's about the plane trip.

It's anxiety, they decided.

And I let them—

So my dad brings home two movies from the video store: *The Wedding Singer* and *Air Force One*. The Wedding Singer is so funny, and at the end everyone on the plane cheers for Adam Sandler when he gets the girl. My parents know I like Adam Sandler movies.

Then my mom sets up a chair in the living room, with another chair in front and one on each side.

"Just sit here, Jason." She calls Jeremy. "Jeremy, come help."

I am sitting here.

"Ten more minutes," my mom is saying. She wants me to sit here for ten more minutes, because they think I am nervous about having to sit still in a plane seat for four hours.

This is the way they got me to ride on elevators when I was young and wouldn't get inside. First we just walked near one. And the next day I pressed the button and watched the doors open. After a few weeks of that, once a week, I just stood inside, but my dad held the doors open. We did that every week for a few months until finally I consented to ride up the elevator to my therapist's office, so after a year we didn't have to walk the twelve flights of stairs. I don't even go to that therapist anymore.

We turn off *Air Force One* as soon as the terrorists hijack the plane and start killing people. My mom is yelling at my dad for his poor choice of movies.

But I know they will keep working on this. My mom always says you have to face your fears. This has nothing to do with being scared to get on an airplane, but it's better than telling them the truth.

I am afraid that Rebecca will see me.

I am going to need some time to figure out how to get out of going to Dallas, Texas, for the Storyboard convention.

But my dad has already bought the tickets.

I always listen to the morning announcements at school.

I like the way the words come out of the loudspeakers. I like the voices that have no bodies, that say things from far away so clearly. I know it is really just the lady in the main office, the one with the hard hair, but without a mouth and a face and eyes that look at me I can hear her better.

Every morning I have to stand at the front of the room by the door, because it is noisy in homeroom. My homeroom teacher leaves a note with instructions, so even if we have a substitute, I am allowed to stand here. I have to stand and face the wall. But I listen. I want to hear the lunch service for today, even though I've read the menu. I want to hear which teachers are absent and which buses are late. I don't like there to be surprises.

This morning I am surprised.

"Our biggest congratulations," Dr. T.'s voice is coming from the PA system. "To sixth grader Jason Blake for winning a creative-writing contest and a trip to the Lone Star State . . . and for those of you who don't know, that's Texas. Have a great time, Jason. And don't forget, Jason, to . . . represent. "

Now he is talking about today's assembly on dental hygiene. Now he is talking about parent-teacher conferences and the eighth-grade field trip to Washington, DC, next month. But Dr. T. got one part wrong. The part about me.

I didn't win anything. My parents just signed me up and this makes me wonder about everything else. My parents had to get permission from the school, from Dr. T., for me to miss next Friday. So they must have explained it to him then. I guess NTs don't listen to each other very well either.

But now, worse than him getting it wrong—everyone knows, and I will have to go.

Everyone in the whole school knows I am going to Texas.

I will never be able to get out of this.

The problem inside my room, inside my house, inside my head, is growing bigger and bigger. The problem that Rebecca will see me at the Storyboard convention in Texas is growing bigger and wider.

All my worlds are colliding.

I never wanted it to happen this way.

When we go to the library, Miss Leno seems very excited, even though a couple of months ago she said I was rude.

"Jason, what wonderful news," she is saying to me. "Don't you want to go on your computer? It's empty. It's waiting for you."

Computers don't wait for people.

But I don't want to go on the computer.

I can't check my e-mail from school. They won't let you, but if they did, I sure wouldn't want to. I didn't respond to Rebecca's message yet, the message that says she is going to the Storyboard convention.

I don't know what to write to her, so I think it's best not to write anything.

I don't know what to tell my dad or my mom. Thing are set into motion, and I can't stop them. Bad things.

When Rebecca sees me, she will not like me anymore.

"Jason?" I hear Miss Leno's voice, but it is behind me now, because I have turned away.

124

I can walk to the window, where I can see the parking lot and the line of trees. I can almost put myself across the asphalt and into the coolness of the woods. I can hear the leaves, every one nearly the same as the one beside it, brushing against each other, and if I listen—

"You need to be doing *something* this period, Jason—"

Listen—

"Jason, have you finished your library project? Why don't you come over here and work on your project?"

Listen, very carefully, I can hear their meaning:

There is nowhere to hide.

Not in the letters.

Not in the words.

Chapter Twenty-two

My parents sit with me on the four chairs lined up in front of the TV for a full twenty-five minutes this night with no movie. Jeremy gets really impatient. He won't wear the make-believe seat belt, and my parents start fighting.

"Jeremy doesn't have to do this," my dad is saying.

"We are a family," my mom says back.

I am watching the TV screen.

Jeremy takes off.

"Wanna read me a story?" Jeremy is asking.

The book he wants me to read to him is open, and Jeremy is sitting in the exact spot, not too close, not too far, next to my pillow.

But I am not in the mood. The feeling I have wraps up my whole body. I can't get it off. I can't get out.

"No," I say.

Jeremy doesn't move. I knew he wouldn't.

"Read," Jeremy says.

Sometimes it feels like there are bugs in my brain, bugs like the ones that bang themselves against our front screen door at night in the summer, when the light is on outside. I can hear their wings spinning, caught inside the glass hood of the lamp, vibrating in desperation.

What will happen when Rebecca sees me?

I have a math test tomorrow. I can't do the math. What will she think of me? My shirt, this shirt, is stained from lunch. Why do I do that? And it is very hot in here. I can't stand it. My skin hurts. All of it.

And Jeremy smells like bubble gum. Why does he smell like bubble gum and ketchup?

Rebecca will not like me the minute she sees me. Like all girls don't.

The bugs throw their buzzing bodies against the screen, in no order, over and over, with no hope. There is no way they can get in, and why would they want to, anyway? What's in here for them?

"Is it because of the bird girl?" Jeremy is asking me. "The one you write to online?"

The tight wrapper around my body loosens when he says that, giving my heart room to breathe.

I nod.

"What about her, Jason?"

I am reading the book, and Jeremy is listening. But I am also telling him. In between pages and pictures the words get tangled up, but Jeremy understands.

"She is going to Dallas, Texas, too?"

"Yes."

"So that's good, isn't it, Jason? Isn't she your girlfriend? Don't you want to see your girlfriend?"

I shake my head. *No.*

Now Jeremy is quiet. He is resting his head on my pillow, right where my head sleeps at night. I smell the ketchup and the bubble gum. Jeremy doesn't move when I slip a piece of his hair between my fingers.

In and out, until one by one all the bugs fly away.

For now. For tonight.

The next day is the beginning of a C schedule, and just like the hard-haired office lady announced, there are Italian dunkers today—my favorite. And garden salad, dinner rolls even though it is lunch, and cherry Jell-O. Usually this food makes me happy, but today I carry my tray across the black-and-white-checkered floor and sit by myself.

There are a million little specks inside the top of this table, specks of color that run so deep into the plastic they seem suspended in space. Colorful snowflakes that never move and never fall.

Bennu can hardly imagine what life would be like as a normal-sized person. His parents, surprisingly, are not pressuring their son. Bennu's father tells him the decision is his to make. *It's your life, Bennu. Your body. We love you, Bennu, no matter what your size, no matter what your limitations.*

His mother cries and cries, but she also agrees to stick with whatever decision Bennu will make. *We want you to be happy, Bennu,* she says. The doctor tells them he will wait three days for an answer, and only three days.

That night Bennu has a dream—

"Jay-Man, come sit with us."

I don't have to look up. I know it is Aaron Miller.

"Hey, man, nobody wants to eat alone," he is saying.

Sometimes I can block out the noises in the cafeteria like my therapist taught me, grab the sound and throw it away like all the food in the garbage can.

The clanking of plates being dropped onto the metal counter.

Grab it and throw it away.

The cafeteria lady, the one with the red bandanna and the yellow teeth, arguing with one of the kids about his lunch card. She says it's not his. He says it is.

Grab it and throw it away.

The sound of the dishwasher, way in the back, humming and steaming, clicking on and off in cycles.

Chairs scraping across the floor.

Paper bags crumpled.

Angry voices.

Happy voices.

Laughing. Whispering.

Nobody wants to eat alone.

"C'mon, Jason," Aaron says again. "Look, nobody else is sitting there. They left already. C'mon. It's just me."

I pick up my tray and follow Aaron's feet. I slide as quietly as I can up to the table. And I watch the lights on the ceiling, which are not one color but made up of all colors and which move and flicker and dance if you pay attention.

If I had the words out loud, in my mouth, the words that told a story, that made a connection, that could draw a picture for Aaron to hear, I could ask him for help. I would ask Aaron what he would do. Aaron is a boy people like. Even when they look at him. And see him. And know who he is.

Bennu—

Who is real but not real, only Aaron does not know this.

I—can see Bennu but not see him.

Bennu is a dwarf.

Who likes a girl, a girl who is average height.
But oh, see now!
There is a cure.
There is a doctor.
An operation he could have.
He has three days.
What should he do?
Aaron is very quiet.

Am I talking? Really talking? Most everyone is gone from the cafeteria. Fewer noises. The lights shutter. The dishwasher far off in the kitchen shuts off.

"Wow, great story," Aaron is saying. "Bennu, huh? So, he decides he is going to have the operation. Scary stuff, man."

Aaron is putting the crumpled paper from his cupcake, the tinfoil from his sandwich, and the stems from his grapes into his paper bag. He is done eating. He pushes his chair out behind him.

He says, "Well, good for Bennu, I guess."

Aaron stands up. He bends his arm all the way back, behind his head, the paper bag in his hand.

He says, "But hey, wouldn't it be weird—if Bennu wakes up from the operation, and he's all tall and stuff, and then he doesn't recognize himself in the mirror?"

I hear Aaron's paper bag hit the plastic rim, and I hear it fall inside.

Chapter Twenty-three

Irony is a trick in literature.

It is very hard to explain what irony really is. It is one of those abstract things like those similarity questions on IQ tests. It can be something someone says or something someone does or something that happens. Irony is when the exact opposite of what is expected happens.

Irony can be used to be funny.

Or to make a point without being obvious.

I wrote a story last year for language arts about a man who was so afraid of dying, getting hurt, or getting ill that he did everything he could to avoid it from happening. He had air machines pump filtered air into his house. He had a special car built for himself that was virtually indestructible. He ate only food that was grown in his special clean-soil-and-water greenhouse. He had every surface in his house padded so he would never get a bruise or a cut. If he ever had to go outside, he wore a specially designed suit that protected him from the other people, objects, the sun, and any polluted air. It even had a lightweight metal helmet in case something fell from one of the other buildings or from the sky. And then one day while he was taking a walk, one of the air hoses in his suit had a malfunction and the man died right there on the street. He suffocated in his own invention that was designed to protect him.

That is irony.

My teacher really liked it, but she said it was a week late, and I got a B minus. That is not ironic, that is just very unfair.

I have sat in a chair pretending to be flying on a plane for a total of one hundred and thirty-seven minutes over the course of this whole week and a half. I wasn't nervous at all about flying before, but now that my dad has told me not to worry about the announcement about the exit row and how the seats can be used as flotation devices, I am a little worried.

"There's nothing to be afraid of," he tells me.

Rebecca.

And I feel my eyes sting.

"I'll be with you the whole time, Jason," my dad tells me. His voice is so soft. I know he loves me, but I can't tell him. I would cry.

Boys are not supposed to cry.

I am scared.

And boys are not supposed to be scared.

This is something he can't fix, like he used to when I was little. When I was little and my dad and mom could make everything all right just by being there. Or saying something. Or telling me what to do. Or making cookies.

My dad can't fix me now. No matter how much he loves me.

So I don't tell him what's wrong, because I don't want him to feel bad about that.

It was ironic, however, that for my fourth birthday, the year my mom signed me up for nursery school, the year Jeremy was born, my dad bought me a toy truck as my present, and I hated it.

It was metal with rubber tires and a light on top that really turned on. The light was red and spun around inside its plastic cover. The metal was cold and sharp, and the light hurt my eyes. It was too big and too small at the same time. It was hard to push along the ground. It hurt my hand, and I couldn't see the fun in that at all. It hurt my knees, too, to be down on the floor pushing this truck.

What I really wanted was a new computer game for my birthday that year.

"Do you love it, Jason?" my dad asked me. "Isn't it cool?"

So then I knew my dad loved the truck. And in that same moment, even though I was only four years old, I knew my dad would be hurt if I didn't—

Like the truck too, as much as he did.

Maybe more.

So I said, "Yeah."

I was just trying to protect my father from having his feelings hurt.

Irony is also when the true meaning of a character's actions or words are clear to the reader but, *ironically*, not to the character himself.

I don't remember very much from nursery school, but I remember the first day, seeing my name spelled out in my cubby. I remember it was all capital letters, and that bothered me. Only the first letter should be capitalized. I wasn't feeling very good about this experience. I didn't want to go inside the room.

I didn't like those letters, but no one else saw it.

I moved forward.

I remember warm apple juice that just smells so bad.

The man who played the guitar that hurt my ears.

And then one day I remember my mother fighting with Miss Baum. My mother's voice was sharp. Miss Baum's voice was scratchy.

"He's fine, Miss Baum," my mother said. "I don't see you

talking to some of these other parents." I felt her arm sweep over my head. I felt the breeze. I heard the music coming from the other room. I remember the music. They were singing "The Wheels on the Bus."

B-A-U-M

B-O-M-B

Miss Baum but not *miss bomb*.

Not like a bomb, Miss Baum. Different spelling but similar personality.

"Some of these other parents," my mother said, "whose kids are so mean. The kids who make fun of other kids. Or how 'bout that Samuel Diamond who won't let my Jason on the climber? And pushed him? Is pushing more normal to you, Miss Baum? Is that more acceptable?"

"Mrs. Blake, I am just suggesting some kind of testing might be a good idea."

"Ridiculous. Unless maybe your eyes need to be tested, Miss Baum. So you can see what's going on in your own classroom."

"Here, Mrs. Blake, if you change your mind. Yale–New Haven. It's not far."

"Ridiculous," my mother said. I felt her hand pull me and pull me away.

I think my only choice is to never write to Rebecca again.

If only I wasn't going to the convention.

It has already been two days. Then Rebecca wrote me again and asked if I got her last message.

Rebecca is a girl. And she is a friend. So I should be answering her notes.

Rebecca is my girlfriend, like I told Aaron, and if I want to keep it that way, I can never talk to her again.

So maybe she'll think I dropped my computer and it's in the shop, or we went away somewhere without Internet. I could be in the hospital. There are many reasons I could think of that a person would never go on their computer ever again.

If only I wasn't going to the convention.

She'll never know, but at least she won't really know.

Another reason is I could be dead.

Now a series of unrelated events occurs.

It rains heavily on the East Coast for five days in a row, and the play-off games scheduled for Boston and New York City are postponed nearly a full week.

The assistant producer at the SportsNow Network, where my dad works, gets a stomachache, throws up three times in one day, stops by the emergency room at St. Vincent's on his way home from work, and is rushed into surgery for an appendectomy.

Our flight to Dallas/Fort Worth is cancelled three days before we are supposed to leave, and the only nonstop flight they can get us on is in two days.

My dad says he can't possibly make it.

Besides, things at work are now very backed up.

My parents are downstairs fighting about it right now. *Family should come before work,* my mother is saying. *It's not my choice,* my dad is saying.

The word that came into my mind this morning while I was brushing my teeth was "serendipity." I have never had my word have so much meaning to what is going on, which in itself is serendipitous. This word I knew already. "Serendipity" means "the occurrence and development of events by chance in a happy or beneficial way."

I am happy and beneficial.

I don't have to go to the convention.

I watch my computer boot up. The blue screen and then my screen saver. The clicks click and the whirls whirl. Even my computer sounds happier.

I will write to Rebecca now. We can stay friends.

`Rebecca, sorry it took me so long to write you back.`

I was thinking of making up a reason I didn't write right away, but I decide against it.

`The ending to your story is really good. I like how`

the people figured out they really needed each other after all. I could see it made into a movie. That's great news about the convention. You won't believe it, but I was almost going to go too. But my dad just found out he has to work that weekend.

This is the best thing that could have happened. It is serendipitous.

Too bad, because that would have been great.

This is just an outright lie.

We could have taken a workshop or something together. Well, have a great time without me.

I am hoping this doesn't sound *too* friendly, but maybe a little cute. I know girls like cute boys.

I hope she cannot read the relief in my words.

I don't want to hurt her feelings. I wonder if my feelings would be hurt if it were the other way around. I think, but I am not sure.

I want her to know I really like her. I want her to think I really *wish* I could go.

I really like Rebecca. She is my girlfriend. Because Rebecca is my girlfriend, that's why I am worried about hurting her feelings.

So I sign my name at the end of the e-mail, but instead of "sincerely" or "yours truly," I write "love."

Love, Jason Blake.

So she will know.

Boy gets girl.

Chapter Twenty-four

We went anyway—

To have me tested at Yale–New Haven like Miss Baum suggested.

Three years later, but we went.

And on the way there my mom got lost.

My dad knocks on my door, so that for a second it seems that when I press send on my computer it makes a knocking sound on my door. That is a coincidence, but I wouldn't exactly call it serendipitous.

My dad comes into my room and tells me, "Good news. We found another flight and the airline is going to transfer my ticket to Mom. We didn't want to tell you until we were sure it could be done. You are still going to the convention!"

I look at my computer screen, where it still flashes YOUR MESSAGE HAS BEEN POSTED.

I don't know what it is. I don't why it is, but for some reason the news doesn't ricochet around my brain. My head stays connected to my body. The air goes inside and comes back out. Nothing happens.

I just pressed send.

"We didn't want to disappoint you, Jason. We know how much this Storyboard thing means to you," my dad says.

I wrote "Love, Jason."

When a person is really happy, you can hear it in their voice. You can feel it in the way they take up space in a room. I know my dad is standing by my door and he is smiling. I have very good vision out of the corners of my eyes.

"And don't worry, Jason," my dad says. "I'll make sure to rent Mom a car with a GPS." He is laughing.

If my dad were a color, it would be orange. Happy. He likes to make me happy.

I would be dark green, like the bottom of the ocean that doesn't get any light from the sun, where the weird-looking organisms live that nobody ever sees. Or maybe I would be one of those creatures, colorless, with skin so translucent you can see right through them. You can see all their organs working inside, bubbling and squeezing, but if you brought them up to the surface they'd die instantly, because they'd be so sensitive to the light. That's why they live down there at the very bottom of the ocean.

But for some reason it is very quiet down here, and I am still, and so I just nod my head.

There was some confusion with the overhead road signs on the way to Yale–New Haven. I remember that, even though it was four years ago.

And there were big, big trucks on either side of us. The directions were printed on a piece of paper that crumpled loudly in her hand that held tight to the steering wheel.

I was still young enough to have to sit in the back strapped into a seat. Jeremy was home with a babysitter.

I was eight.

The more nervous my mother got, the more I rocked into a rhythm so I couldn't hear her words. But I heard them anyway.

Why does Yale have to be in New Haven?

Was that just the exit?

Jason, stop that. Just sit still. We are fine.

Oh, jeez, where did that truck come from?

Why isn't your father with me when I need him?

It was almost as confusing to find the building and then the elevator and then the office with the right name on the door. DR. MARAKESH.

And I spelled it over and over in my head as we sat in the soft seats with the rough fabric that hurt my skin.

"What's wrong with him?"

"Pardon me?" I heard my mother's voice.

"His mouth is moving, but he's not saying anything."

"Where is your mother, little girl?" My mother told the little voice, "Don't you think you should go sit with your mother?"

"I'm autistic," the little-girl voice said. "And I bet he is too."

So I am going to the Storyboard convention again.

After all that.

It is very ironic.

But not the least bit funny.

Placate.

That's the word that came to me this morning, as we were getting ready to leave for the airport. I was brushing my teeth really hard, even though the dentist told me I brush my teeth too hard. Sometimes I forget.

We are getting ready to go to JFK Airport and then fly to DFW, Dallas/Fort Worth. In Texas, where the convention is. Where Rebecca lives.

Placate.

I know what that word means.

It has nothing to do with what's going on.

Inside the John F. Kennedy Airport, JFK, the sound is bad.

Like the gym at school, only worse. The ceiling is so far, too high, and the noise travels up there and sticks like an invisible thick cloud. Except here in the airport there are rows and rows and lines and lines and hall after hall and there is a lot of noise that gets stuck up there. There are conversations everywhere. Constant loudspeakers speaking.

I pull my mother out of the way of a huge speeding golf cart that is screaming with a high-pitched warning, only with all the noise in this place there was no warning at all.

"I think you just saved my life," my mother is saying.

The giant golf cart with the flashing light on top, carrying a little girl with crutches and two old people, passes us by.

I can feel my mother's skin, her fingers. Her arm is bent and stiff. She is nervous too, and we aren't even driving yet. We didn't even have to drive to get here. My dad had someone from his office drive us. But she is already nervous.

Maybe we should have practiced walking through the airport. It is apparently much more stressful than sitting on a plane will be.

All the sounds gather at the ceiling, where there are large white pipes. The voices of all these people, steps large and light, rolling wheels, constant mechanical clicking, beeping, and dinging. This must be what it is like inside my computer.

"He doesn't have an ID. He's only twelve," my mother is

telling the ticket man behind the tall counter. "Yeah, well, he looks big for his age."

Soon my ID will say:

JASON BLAKE

WESTON, CONNECTICUT

STORYBOARD MEMBER

THREE YEARS

Rebecca, in my awake dream, will know who I am, because my identification will be hanging right there around my neck.

But I see Rebecca first.

She is wearing a name tag too, of course. I know it is her, before she sees it is me. She is leaning over the sign-in table gathering her information: the schedule of workshops, the times for the lectures, the room assignments, and coupons for the local outlet shops. When she stands up, I see her face.

I see her face.

There is a large purplish stain across her left cheek and down her neck; that's all I see. It looks like she is two different colors. It is a birthmark like Mr. Shupack has on his arm, but this is all over her face.

It's all I can see when I look at her.

And then I wonder maybe if Rebecca was just as afraid of me seeing her as I am of her seeing me.

Chapter Twenty-five

The GPS in the rental car isn't working.

Or my mom doesn't know how to work it.

If she tries to reverse the car back into the parking lot to ask for help, she will run over those metal spikes and pop all the tires, and we would be stuck here for hours.

I kind of hope that happens.

I am not looking forward to getting to the hotel.

Because then I will be that much closer to the convention.

That much closer to Rebecca seeing me.

My mother has never really been the same since we left Yale–New Haven that afternoon.

And I, apparently, never had been.

The doctor asked me questions and gave me puzzles to do. They made me look at patterns and then asked me to draw them. They gave me blocks. And pictures. They tried to get me to think we were playing fun games, board games and word games and stacking games.

But nothing was fun.

They gave me numbers and told me to repeat them.

"One. Seven. Eight. Five."

They told me riddles and asked me to explain them. They showed me photographs of faces and asked me what the person was feeling.

"Is this person happy or sad?"

They showed me pictures of clothing and asked me who would wear this?

"Who would wear this dress?"

I cried and tried to run away. They gave me candy, and I played more games. I drew more pictures. I recited more numbers.

Then they talked to my mom, and I got to play video games or watch TV in a special waiting room, not the one we waited in when we first came in. There were lots of other kids in this room and maybe some grown-up watching. But the grown-up didn't seem connected to any particular kids. There were five or six video machines, some like in an arcade and another hooked up to a little television set that wasn't even in color. There were books on the table and some on the floor. There were headsets on all the video games, but you could still hear the music and the beeping and the chiming if one of the kids didn't have the earpiece on his head right.

And there were a lot more kids than there were video games.

I stood ready for this kid to get down from the stepping stool so I could have a turn next. Every time he looked like he was going to get off, he'd look at me and play again.

My head started to fly off my body. I wanted a turn. I wanted to play.

One of the grown-ups came over and stood near me. Tall legs and a man's voice.

"It's okay, Jason. I will make sure you have a turn. I have a watch. See?"

A little clock came down in front of my face. *It's not a watch; it's a clock. How can I trust this voice?*

I will never have a turn.

But just then a woman's voice came through the opened door, and the little kid at the video game ran away. I stepped up onto the stool as fast as I could. I don't remember what the game was. It was old and it wasn't that interesting, but I grabbed on to it so I wouldn't fly away.

When my mother came into the room through the opened door, I looked at her face. I never look at her face. I am afraid to look at her face. But all the strange shoes and the unknown voices, the games and the noises. The candy was sick in my stomach.

I looked at her face.

She had been crying.

Her face was so ugly, red, and puffy.

She is so ugly because she is so mad at me, I thought.

Because I would not end my video game and get down from the stool, and because I wet my pants, all down my legs and into my shoes—

My mother is crying.

"It will be okay, Jason," my mother is saying. I can hear the crying just waiting inside her voice. She has pulled the rental car over in order to reprogram the GPS.

She is clicking and spinning.

Then she is making noises from her mouth. Now her hands are around her head, in her hair, like she tells me not to do. She is not putting in the right letters. The computer can't help you if you don't ask it the right question.

I can.

I can reach over.

I can spell the exact name of the hotel. The arrow points to each letter. You have to spin the dial. It turns smooth in my hands, clicks into each spot, drops like pennies in a jar. The letters spill into my hands, out my fingers. Return to enter. *H.* Enter. *E.* Back to start. All the letters click into place. Smooth. The hotel is spelled out, and the mechanical voice starts talking.

"Proceed to the route shown," it says. It sounds like a girl's voice.

I can feel my mother's shoulder drop. I know she wants to reach over and hug me and really let herself cry.

I am glad she is driving and can't do this.

"Jason," she says. I can tell by the sound of her voice that she is keeping her head facing forward. "Thank you, thank you, my sweetheart." She is looking at the road ahead instead of at me.

A couple of days after we got back from Yale–New Haven they told me I was autistic, but they didn't really use that word.

Autistic.

I didn't learn that word until a long time later. First my mom and dad told me I was special. I had a different way of seeing the world and a different way of being in the world.

"And now we know how to get real help," my dad said. "The right kind. Everything is going to be better now, Jason."

"Now we know what's going on, Jason," my mother said. "Now we know what's wrong. And so we can fix it."

They told me the word for what was wrong, three letters, and it gave me a name. My mom and dad were saying something. They were telling me things. But at eight years old I had already learned that people will say one thing and mean something else completely.

Special.

Different.

But in a way I was relieved.

It explained some things, like why none of the other kids minded sitting in the grass when Mrs. Babcock took us outside on sunny days. The grass felt like needles. I hate to sit on the ground. I like to stand.

It explained things like why Henry Gaberman told me my face was like a blinking traffic signal.

Like why I didn't really have any friends who invite me to their house after school.

But I didn't think anything was going to get any better.

I didn't need any letters or any new names to tell me what I already knew.

It is so hot in Dallas.

Hot like sticky wool on my skin.

When we get out of the car and walk to the hotel, I feel like I am swimming in a horribly heated pool. I have to walk fast, my pants legs swishing against each other. My mother is a lot slower, and when the automatic doors of the hotel shut behind me, she is still on the other side.

And all of a sudden I am inside by myself.

Is this what it feels like to be alone in a strange place?

I don't know what to do. There are people in line at the counter, people walking around. People who work in the hotel all wear dark purple jackets. A woman has a suitcase on wheels. Another woman is pushing a stroller. A man in a chair, like this is his living room, reading a newspaper. Down one hall a little kid is crying. I smell the chlorine of a pool, but I don't see one. I smell the chemical odor of carpet glue. The elevator makes a noise just before it lands and opens wide.

There is a drinking fountain by the restrooms. A urinal is still flushing when the men's-room door flings open and swings closed. A phone rings. Two phones ring, and neither one is picked up.

"Jason, Jason. Stop that. Stop that."

I don't know what I am doing, but my mother is mad at me for doing it.

"C'mon," she says.

I follow her pink and white sneakers and the tall rolling suitcase that stays right beside her.

She gives the man behind the counter our name. She gives him her credit card. He gives her a key, which looks like another credit card.

"C'mon, Jason," she says.

And I do.

I think I could live very well in a hotel room. There are so few choices. And so little furniture. It's pretty quiet for the most part unless you turn the volume on the TV too loud.

And turn it up and then down.

You can read the temperature on the thermostat, and nobody gets too mad if you turn that up or down, unless you keep doing it.

And the windows don't open in a hotel room. I like that, too.

But I've never been in a hotel room with just my mom. She

seems different, like without my dad she isn't the same.

I understand that.

There are some things my dad always does. Like give the man who brought our suitcases up some money. My mother fumbled around. She didn't know what the man in the uniform was waiting for.

Then she didn't know how much to give him.

"Two," I told her. I always watch my dad. I knew how much to give.

And there are things my dad could never do. My dad could never cook dinner and help me with my math homework and play Uno with Jeremy all at the same time. My mom does that.

Placate.

Serendipity.

Confluence.

Vizcaíno.

Jaba Chamberlain.

"It's strange being in a hotel without Daddy and Jeremy, isn't it?" she says to me.

Most things are strange to me, I am thinking.

Chapter Twenty-six

Before I walk into a room where there are going to be a lot of people, like the room where the registration for the convention is, there are certain things I am supposed to do. My occupational therapist taught me what to do.

I am supposed to touch the wall of the doorway with the backs of both my hands, and press. As hard as I can. For ten seconds, counting quietly in my mind.

Not out loud.

I am supposed to have a destination when I walk in, so I am not just wandering around, which can make me anxious.

I am supposed to anticipate being overwhelmed.

I am supposed to listen to my own breathing and know it's in my control. And I am supposed to keep my eyes just a few feet in front of me, like car headlights.

Breathe.

Don't drive over your own headlights.

Though even my therapist could not have anticipated this.

Right as we walk in, there is a historical fight demonstration going on. The two actors are dressed as warriors from the olden days, the days of kings and queens. They are fighting with long swords. The noise is really loud, metal against metal. The men are grunting. Their beards are falling off. They are sweating into their costumes. I can smell them from here.

A young woman walks by dressed like Hermione, and there are about fifteen Harry Potters all over the room. A lot of the characters I don't recognize from any book or television show.

But I can't look very carefully.

I have to concentrate, breathe, and think only of the space directly in front of me. Then directly in front of me is a blur of beads and black hair. I think it is Captain Jack Sparrow.

But my therapist didn't anticipate Rebecca either.

Everything happens just the same as in my last awake dream. The lady in the sign-in line even takes the same few steps just to get farther away from me. And when I sign in, I get my name tag, which is not the sticky peel-off kind but a real one in a plastic sleeve that hangs on an elastic cord to put around your neck.

And my dad gets one too. Only now it is my mom.

I look down at the tag hanging around my neck.

JASON BLAKE

WESTON, CONNECTICUT

STORYBOARD MEMBER

THREE YEARS

"Excuse me. But can you tell me if I am in the right line?"

A girl has stepped up beside me. I smell her first, in the air like baby powder. Her shampoo is strawberry. She reaches out with one hand toward the table. In her other hand she has a cane.

"My name is Rebecca," she says. "Am I in the right line to get my name tag?"

She doesn't know, because she can't see. Nothing here is in Braille, and Rebecca is blind.

My father is wrong.

There is such a thing as luck.

The man dressed like Jack Sparrow from *Pirates of the Caribbean* rushes by me, shouting, "Ahoy!"

I press the backs of both my hands against the door frame for ten seconds.

"To yourself," my mother reminds me.

I count to myself.

My mother is right next to me when we walk into the Perdinalez Room where the Storyboard registration is being held. There is a black bulletin board on an easel with white letters, plastic letters, that spell out:

WELCOME STORYBOARD WRITERS

AND THEIR FAMILIES

This is another thing that always worries me. I worry that I am not in the right place. We are in the right place.

But so far I don't see anyone with a Seeing Eye dog—or a birthmark.

—nobody smells like strawberries and baby powder.

Not that I really expect to.

There was only one table for signing in.

There was no line of people. There were no hanging plastic identification cards. There was a sheet of sticky labels, and you had to write your own name. There were three permanent markers; two were missing their caps, the red and the black.

"Your name, Jason. You're supposed to write your name there." My mom hands me the blue marker.

Of course I know this.

My name.

How can I get out of doing this?

"Jason, your name. Write your name."

My mother still speaks louder when she thinks I don't understand or that I'm not listening.

What am I looking for?

"Jason, what are you smelling? Your name. Just write your name. Do you want me to do it?"

My mother takes the red marker, but it is almost dried out. She writes in a light shade with blank streaks that should be red.

JASON BLAKE.

Love, Jason Blake.

"Here you go," my mother says. She very gently presses the name tag to my shirt. "And can you loosen your belt . . . just a notch, maybe?"

Chapter Twenty-seven

"Are you Jason? Blake? From Connecticut? There aren't many other kids here. Not like . . . our age, anyway."

I don't have to see her.

I don't have to look at her face. I don't have to answer. I know that it is her.

And she smells like strawberries.

"Who are you?" my mother is asking.

"Oh, I am Rebecca Stone. Jason told me he wasn't going to be here . . . but look. You're here." Her voice is so real. I am awake. I am not dreaming. I can hear her.

"He *told* you?" my mother is saying. I can feel her shaking hands with someone. "You two know each other?" Beside me my mother's body is shifting slightly as her hand is moving up and down. They are shaking hands.

"From the computer," she says. Like singing.

I tell my body what to do. I twist my head far ahead and I let my arm do what it is supposed to. I put my hand out to shake.

This is Rebecca, and she smells like strawberries.

"Are you . . . *Jason?*" she is asking. Her hand is dry, and I feel her skin, her bones. Her hand. I feel her skin and I smell her shampoo. I focus on the wall by the tables.

I am nodding. *Yes, I am Jason.*

"I'm Jason's mother," my mother says. "Elizabeth Blake."

"I'm Rebecca," Rebecca says. She said that already, but I can't look at her face. I am supposed to look. To try.

I want.

I want.

I want to be a snowflake that blends in with all the rest of the snow. So nobody really knows what it looks like.

So badly.

But now my mother is talking, but I can't listen to what she is saying, something about where we are from. The plane. The computer. Oh, the computer. Of course. Storyboard. Of course. Yes, Jason has a little brother.

Then my mother says, "So you're a writer, too? Jason is a great writer."

"I know," Rebecca says. "I love Jason's stories," she says, but her voice has already changed. She sounds more like a grown-up. It is nice but not nice. It is not for me. It is for her. It is for my mother. Rebecca changed the letters when I wasn't watching. She changed the language when I was trying to look back from the wall.

I can look *next* to Rebecca. I can see her brown hair and the tall folding screen where there are posters and sign-up sheets and more people. There is a man and woman arguing by the door. I see the round of Rebecca's cheek and her eyelashes, but I can't even smell her shampoo anymore.

I want so badly to breathe.

I want.

But I am the same.

Look in the mirror—

I am still the same.

Boy loses girl.

Chapter Twenty-eight

I started hearing the word "autistic" a lot after my diagnosis in third grade. But I didn't know if it was one of those things like when you learn a new word and all of sudden you see it everywhere. And you don't know if that's because you didn't know the word before so you never noticed it, or because all of sudden it's everywhere.

Some numbers you outgrow. They stick to you for a while, and then you move on. Like your age and your grade. But some stay with you, like your birthday. Maybe your favorite baseball player if he never got traded.

Letters are like that too.

The letters of your name never change, unless you grow up and get famous and you want a different kind of name.

But your real name never changes.

And people will always look you up and find out your real name.

I knew I had these new letters—ADOS, LD, HFA, PDD–NOS—that would always be linked to my name, that I was not going to outgrow. And even if my mom didn't know it, I only had one choice. I could keep my name with all its letters and sounds and all its meaning and all its nonmeaning. Or I could disappear.

And that's when I started writing stories.

My mother is talking loudly on her cell phone. She says the hotel will charge us money to use their phone. But there is not very good reception, so she has to stand in the little hall by the closet. Otherwise I think she would be in the bathroom with the door closed so I couldn't hear her.

Because she is not telling the truth.

"No, no, everything is fine. How's Jeremy? Did he eat the meat loaf I left you guys? No, no, we found the place just fine and we are all checked in. We registered about an hour ago. Yeah, there are lots of workshops Jason is interested in. It's great. Just great."

My mom is a lot like me. She doesn't want the people she loves to worry. She doesn't want them to be sad.

The air conditioner in this room vibrates, like a piece of metal inside is loose. I like it. I am standing right next to it, listening. The pitch rises and falls like a voice, only this voice is calm and it is telling me to relax. I am comfortable slipping into this humming voice and talking to it in return.

I have a lot of feelings but nothing to say.
All the letters and all the words they form escape me.

I never finished my Bennu story. I was going to write the ending and then post it so Rebecca would read it before she went to the Storyboard convention.

After I found out I wasn't going.

Before I found out I was going again.

But now I never want to write.

I never want to put words together, and sounds, and letters. That have meaning and that don't. Sounds like poetry and like weapons.

That hurt, and wound and lie, and those that fly. And soar. In which I find freedom. There will be no more.

I want to go home.

I don't want to be here.

These are the awake dreams that are real. Like the bad dreams that are more real.

Like having no dreams at all. I will never write again.

But my mom orders us room service and we get to eat dinner in our twin beds and watch *Law and Order*. Then we brush our teeth and go to sleep.

Bennu is my last fictional character. There will not be more. It was my last story ever. Bennu will have the last word.

No one will ever hear him.

Not even I will.

Chapter Twenty-nine

We order the breakfast buffet in the morning.

On other trips with my family we don't.

Because, my mother says, it is too expensive and we could never eat enough food to justify that kind of money. But I think my mother is trying to make me feel better this morning.

And that's nice.

What's also nice is that she still hasn't tried to talk to me. Or make me talk to her. She hasn't asked me about Rebecca. Who she was. How I knew her.

There are seven different kinds of cold cereals in those miniature boxes. Someone lined them up like play blocks. Under those metal covers are scrambled eggs, two kinds of bacon, French toast, and hash browns. The covers are hot when you lift them up. Steam hits you in the face.

The person behind me with her plate in her hand is waiting.

She waits until I am all done looking at everything. She hasn't come a step closer, even though there is room.

There are three rows of juice glasses, red, orange, and yellow. I don't know what the yellow one is.

"Cranberry, orange, and I don't know," my mother is saying.

We sit down at a table, with cloth napkins and coffee cups and silverware.

"Yes, please," my mother says when the coffeepot comes to our table. I watch my mother turn her cup right side up. The coffee sounds like a waterfall.

"Do you think you're ready for session one, Jason? It starts in about an hour," she is asking me. Her cup clinks back into the saucer.

Session one.

I signed up for Turning Fact into Fiction before we even got here, when we had to fill out the registration online, but I don't feel like going to it now. I haven't told my mother that I'm never going to write any more stories.

But I'm not.

There is no reason to go the writing workshop.

There isn't anything left.

Why tell a story if there is no one there to read it? Why make a sound if no one will hear it?

Now I am thinking of black paint all over my ceiling at home, covering up all those letters, all those letters twisting themselves into words that nobody understands anyway.

This was the first morning no word came to me while I was brushing my teeth.

Nothing.

I am a blank.

My mother is looking away. There is something about the way the skin on her face is loose now. Her hands are on the table; even her fingers are loose. If she were a color, she would not be bright right now. She would not have much color.

I think she is sad.

"What, Mom?" I ask her.

When she looks up, I am still looking at her.

"I just love you so much, Jason," she tells me. "When you hurt, I hurt."

L-O-V-E.

I can feel her love around me. Like colors and letters taking shape, some I can see and some that are still moving. Some I know, some I don't. They stand still long enough to give a name. I want to name what I am feeling. Love is like yellow. Warm and safe.

"Grapefruit," I say.

I want to say something. I love my mom so much.

She says, "Yes, I think it is. Grapefruit juice."

I make a face. I pinch my face.

"Yeah. Too sour for me, too."

Then, just as we are about to leave the restaurant, I see Rebecca Stone walking in. I don't recognize her face exactly, but I know who she is.

Maybe it's the way my mother stiffens.

But probably more I put it together when Rebecca suddenly stops walking, then bends down to the carpeted floor like she has to tie her shoe, which doesn't need to be tied at all, then she suddenly stands, turns, and walks in the exact opposite direction. And then when the woman who was walking with her notices that Rebecca is no longer with her, she calls out, "Rebecca, where are you going? Breakfast is this way."

I wonder if Rebecca has seen me or maybe she forgot something outside or in her car. And who is that woman with her? I think maybe it is her mother.

At the same instant I am thinking all this, I hear a funny little sound. It reminds me of Lester, when he was alive. But when he was sick and you'd go to pet him. He'd make this funny little sound that only comes from pain, I think. Now it comes from my mother's mouth.

It is not the kind of sound you can mistake for anything else.

Bennu drives all day to get to the hospital the day of his big operation. The directions are complicated, and the driver gets lost a couple of times in the high mountains that rise above the village where Bennu has lived all his life with his family. But because Bennu is so small, he has noticed the different types of soil and dirt, and he is able to direct the driver to just the right ravine, and right to the hospital.

There is a nurse at the station who takes his name and all his information. Just in case.

"Next of kin?" she asks Bennu.

He gives the nurse the names of his mother and father.

"Okay then, well, we just need to run some tests before we begin," the nurse tells Bennu.

"What kind of tests?"

"Oh, don't worry. We do this to everyone."

Bennu doesn't believe that for one minute.

In the first testing room Bennu can't get up onto the examination table. In the second room Bennu can't reach the paper and pencil he is supposed to write on. In the third room Bennu can't press the pedals of the testing machine.

"Okay, now it's time for your operation," the nurse says. "You're going to be just fine."

Bennu isn't too sure about that either.

But he has paid his money and he figures he'd better just go through with it.

"Take a deep breath," the doctor says, "and count to ten." At least Bennu thinks it was the doctor; he didn't recognize him with the mask over his mouth and nose. His voice is muffled too. So Bennu hopes for the best as he counts. *One. Two. Three. Four.*

The next thing Bennu knows, he is in the recovery room. He feels fine. He feels the same as he always did, the same as he is used to. He decides to get out of bed and walk over to the mirror that is hanging by the bathroom door.

But when he swings his feet over the side . . .

What? What is this?

His feet touch the ground while he is still sitting on the bed. Bennu reaches his hands out as far as they would go, and he nearly knocks the clock right off the bedside table.

As quick as he can, he runs over to the mirror.

But of course all he can see is his face.

And his face looks exactly the same.

Oh, no, Bennu cries. *It didn't work. It didn't work. I am the same.*

I am the same.

Chapter Thirty

I used to play baseball.

I used to get invited to birthday parties.

I threw away my baseball glove. I shoved it deep down in the trash can so my mom and dad wouldn't see it.

I used to write stories, but now I know I won't do that anymore either.

Last year my dad was the coach of my Fall Ball baseball team. I liked the way that sounded.

It rhymes. Fall Ball.

So I agreed to play one more season.

We were the SeaHawks, and we got gray T-shirts with the name of MARIO'S PIZZERIA on the back. And a cartoon drawing of a hand holding up a piece of pizza with three pieces of pepperoni on it. And a number.

Thirty-nine.

Of course games were bad, but even in practice I know my dad heard things too.

Jason, why do you run funny like that?

Catch the ball. You're supposed to catch the ball.

What's the matter with him? What's the matter with you?

I heard someone, I think it was a man, tell my dad it was dangerous to have me out there. Way out there. I was in left field. I was always in left field.

"He could get hurt out there," the other dad was saying. "He doesn't pay attention. A fly ball could hit your son right in the head if you're not careful."

I thought about that.

And I stood in the grass. I didn't really like grass, but my dad asked me to stand there. The balls rolled past the kids in gray T-shirts who stood in the dirt. A ball couldn't fly, could it?

No ball came out here in the grass with me.

I didn't hit the ball. I didn't like to step on the hard dirty base. I didn't run right. I didn't stand right. I didn't like the socks. But the pants were soft and had an elastic waist; they were okay.

Sometimes we sat in the dugout.

I sat there a lot.

On a bench. Kids stuck their empty paper water cups in the fence and they stayed there like pimples. One boy kicked the dirt around on home plate, making a cloud around his feet. My dad and his assistant were getting the equipment out of the shed.

My dad left the key in his car.

"Wait here, Jason," he told me.

The dugout was shady. It smelled like bubble gum and fake leather and mud.

"Wanna dead leg?" The voice was a boy's. He was next to me, but his face was turned in the opposite way. Toward the boy on his other side, the one with the long blond hair. I thought that boy was a girl. He had long hair, and girls have long hair.

But it turned out he was a boy.

The boy/girl answered, "No, why don't you give him one instead?" He moved his body farther down the bench.

A dead leg?

"Yeah, why not?"

I heard the thud first. On my body. My eyes flew up to the ceiling. Inside-out shingles. Dark, it was dark, but I could see there were nails sticking into the air. They were bent toward the wood but sticking out, so if you jumped really high you could touch the pointy ends. Then the pain in my leg, so that muscle went hard like a fist hitting me from the inside. Pain.

I had to get away.

I had already learned that if you don't get away, it happens again.

I stood.

But I couldn't. I had only one leg left.

I had a dead leg.

Then there was dirt on my face. And feet. Black shoes. I was looking at the side of the dugout, a blank wall.

"Hey, look, I gave Jason a dead leg. He's dead."

I'm dead?

I felt another thud on my back. I kept staring at the wall.

And another, like hammer on nails. There were more voices and more hammers. Until I was crying. And until I heard my dad.

I heard my dad.

And I heard the other man.

And they were shouting, but I was inside that wall.

Where it was safe.

Loud. Shouting. Crying. Fear. Sadness. Loudness. Fear. Shouting.

Shouting fear.

My leg didn't hurt at all anymore.

"Liz, boys . . . they are just little boys."

"Boys? Those are monsters. If those are boys—"

"I'm not saying it's right. But boys do that kind of stuff to each other. It could have been anyone."

"Not to anyone! Not to anyone! My God, he has bruises."

But my back didn't hurt anymore either.

"Liz, Jason is fine. He'll be fine. Unfortunately, this is the world we live in."

I was only eleven, but I already knew my dad was wrong. There are many, many different worlds to live in. And sometimes there is no connection from one to another.

It's like places where bridges used to be but they got washed away.

Where kids once played baseball but now they don't.

Because they are sorry they blew out the candles when it was someone else's birthday cake. *And now they don't get invited to birthday parties anymore.*

And sorry they pushed over the potter's wheel.

So they tried to write stories so someone would hear them.

But now they don't.

The don't write anymore either.

So when we get back from the buffet, my mother says it's time to get ready to go to the Turning Fact into Fiction Writer's Workshop. I stop moving my feet. I look at the wall in the hallway of our hotel, where I am not home. I grow into the floor and the floor into me.

Rebecca has finally seen me and suddenly not seen me at all. What's the point of going to the workshop when I am never going to write again?

Or play baseball.

I am growing a list, in my feet in the floor, of things I will never do again. Be invited to my cousin Seth's bedroom. Or a birthday party for someone who isn't forced to invite me, like my cousin Seth.

I never liked baseball.

Or my cousin Seth.

I may never use a potter's wheel again in my whole life. But so what? Clay smells really bad. And I will never write another story, so why should I go to the writer's workshop?

And then my mother tells me I don't have to go if I don't want to. And I start to walk again.

"I don't want to go." I repeat what she has just said.

"No, Jason. I understand. We can just watch TV the rest of this morning, if you want. I understand."

"Understand."

"Yes," she says. "Maybe I never really did before."

We are heading back to our room so my mom can use the bathroom.

"I'm not going to make you go to the workshop, Jason," my mom is saying. "If you really don't want to."

She is feeding the room card into the metal slot in our door. The light blinks red. She flips the card over, but the light is still red. She does it again. Red. She jiggles the door anyway, but it will not open. It is still locked.

"Here," I say. It is so easy.

When I slip the card in the right way, the light turns green and my mother can open the door. I made my mother happy because I knew how to open the door.

So I say, "I'll go."

She is heading right for the bathroom, but she looks at me and smiles. "Are you sure, Jason? I mean . . ."

"Sure," I tell her. It's so easy. To make her smile.

And besides, I don't have to write anything. I can just sit there.

I'm good at that.

It is in the Corral Room on the second-floor mezzanine.

I count to ten and press my hands against the sides of the doorway, but there are only five people in the room, and they seem to be sitting as far apart from each other as they can. The room is set up with round tables and chairs. No two people are at the same table.

"This is Turning Fact into Fiction, isn't it?" someone is asking.

"That's what the flyers say up at the desk."

"Flyers? There are flyers?"

My mother says, "Here, Jason. Take a seat and I'll get one of the flyers."

I don't like this room. It is tight, like a room that's been cut in half. The air conditioner blows from the ceiling in one direction, right into the middle of the room. Nobody is sitting at that table.

I don't want to sit there either.

"What's wrong, Jason?"

I am not going to write anymore. I don't want to turn any facts into fiction any more than I want to go and visit Uncle Bobby again anytime soon. Stories and dreams.

But real is worse.

Real is me.

I think when I get home I will delete Storyboard completely from my hard drive. I will throw away all my story files.

"Jason, just sit here. I'll be right back," my mother is saying. "Is it your father? Would it be better if your father were here? He'd know what to do."

She is talking like she always does, sort of to no one, because I know she is not expecting me to answer. "I wonder what time it is. What time is this supposed to start?"

"The instructor is an author," someone at the next table is saying.

"I never heard of him," someone answers.

"He's not so famous, but I heard he's a good teacher. Maybe they're just signing autographs."

My mom comes back with the flyer. But I don't look at it. But I do sit down, in each chair at the table, one, two, three, four, and my mother follows me until we stop at after the fifth move. On this side the air doesn't touch me.

I am facing the wall.

"All good now, Jason?" my mother asks me. "Good."

Nobody in the whole room is talking, and you can hear the buzzing from the overhead lights. And the air conditioner sucking up all my stories, every word and every letter. I wonder if there is a buffet for lunch, too.

"Sorry, so sorry." The voice comes from behind me. If I turn I will see, but I face the wall, letting all stories leave my head, the way my therapist told me to control the noise. *Grab each one and let it go.*

Grab each one and let it go.

The man in the protective suit.

The girl in a world where no one needs anyone.

Bennu.

Rebecca.

PhoenixBird.

Let them go.

The voice of the instructor makes its way to the front of the room. "Well, it's a small group. So what do you say we all move forward? Maybe we can even fit at one table."

I will not move.

The stories come apart like in a movie that is run backward. The characters crumble, first their heads, their hands and arms and feet, and the bodies. The paragraphs melt. The sentences fall apart. And then each word floats alone without any connection. And finally the letters, each letter that without another beside it is completely meaningless.

And I am facing a blank wall.

Coincidences in stories aren't a good idea unless the coincidence sets the plot in motion in the first place or makes things worse for the main character. But at some point in your story things are supposed to get better or be over in some way. The main character is supposed to get what he wants or needs or not.

And then that's the resolution.

But your readers will feel tricked if you just drop something in your story to tie things up, like if all of a sudden the hero finds a pair of magic glasses, or magic candy, or if the long-lost brother they never knew they had shows up and saves the day.

Believability is the key to a good story.

"Come on, people," the instructor is calling. I see hands waving out of the corner of my eye, but something is not right. The hands are not where they should be.

And so I look.

I turn my head, I shift my body, and I raise my eyes, and the instructor is there, standing at the front of the room. He is talking and telling everyone to move their seats.

He is friendly and he lets me breathe.

And then I see. Like a little tiny bridge.

I see that the instructor is a Little Person.

He is a dwarf.

Chapter Thirty-one

Our dwarf instructor from Turning Facts into Fiction is named Hamilton.

"What is the most important part of a writer's body?" he asks the class, which I think is kind of interesting coming from a dwarf. He wrote his name on the dry-erase board that stands beside him.

Hamilton. I don't know if that is his first or last name.

But that's all he wrote.

Maybe it's both. Hamilton Hamilton.

By this time four more people have come into the room. None of them is Rebecca, but now another woman is sitting at the table with me and my mom.

She is the first one to answer. She raises her hand, but she just starts talking at the same time anyway.

"Their heart," she says.

"Good answer," Hamilton says. "But not the one I am looking for. Not the most essential. There are lots of writers with no heart at all."

Some people laugh, but I don't, because that is true.

I am listening.

What is the most important part of a writer's body?

Someone else says, "Hands."

Someone else says, "Your brain."

Then fingers, eyes, ears.

I think about all these things. I know my brain is different from most people, from NTs. I know my hands sometimes fly around the room like they have something to say all on their own. I hear things differently. My eyes are different. I see things and I don't see things.

But I can write. I know I can.

So I jump out of my seat. I stand up. And all those things are loose inside me, like letters of the alphabet that have no meaning until they are all put together.

In one particular way that no one else can do.

In one moment. In one voice. That is mine.

"My bottom!" I say out loud.

And it gets very quiet in the room. Everyone stops calling out answers, and they are all looking at me the way they do in school sometimes, just before everyone starts to laugh. Like in art class, and in gym class. Not the nice kind of laugh.

My mother is looking at me too. She looks like she will punch anyone who laughs.

But Hamilton, the dwarf teacher, says, "Exactly!"

He points right at me. "You've got to sit down on your bottom and *write*. Writing is all we have," he says.

I don't look away. I look right at him.

"All we are, all we can be, are the stories we tell," he says, and he is talking as if he is talking only to me. "Long after we are gone, our words will be all that is left, and who is to say what really happened or even what reality is? Our stories, our fiction, our words will be as close to truth as can be. And no one can take that away from you."

Nobody.

We see Rebecca Stone one more time before we leave Dallas, Texas. It is at the party, that same night, for all the Storyboard conventioneers.

My mom had packed me a blue jacket, white shirt, and khaki pants. I like how I look but I am not very comfortable.

My mom doesn't even tell me to loosen my belt.

I have already thought that Rebecca is probably going to be there too.

"Almost ready?" my mom calls into the bathroom. I stand in front of the mirror looking at myself.

I try to make my face as still as possible.

I try to look at who I am.

But a mirror is not a true representation of a person. It is not. It is reflection. It is the reverse, a pure opposite. They say if a person really saw their own face, they wouldn't recognize themselves. Even a photograph is not a true representation. It is only two-dimensional, while human beings are three-dimensional.

We never really ever see ourselves the way other people see us.

I will just do the best I can.

Rebecca walks right up to us at the party.

She doesn't put out her hand, but she says, "Hi, Jason."

She has a nice voice. I say hi back.

"Did you go to any of the workshops? I did. It was great. I just . . . I wanted to tell you something."

And my mother says, "I can go get some . . . thing. From over there. I'll be back. I'll be over there."

And my mother leaves.

I want to tell Rebecca about Hamilton and about the workshop and the flyers, and about my bottom. I want to ask her to be my girlfriend. I want to tell her that she smells like strawberries and baby powder, and I can't say anything.

I think I know what she will say anyway.

She will say no.

"I like your stories, Jason. When you get back home, I hope you still write me sometimes. I hope I can still send you my stories. You really help me. Did I tell you I got an A on that story you helped me with? Oh, gotta go. There's my mom."

And Rebecca walks away from me.

And that's my story.

Chapter Thirty-two

On the plane ride home my mom says I am wrong.

She says the instructor was not a dwarf at all.

"He's just short, Jason." My mother tells me. "Not all men are tall like your daddy."

"Mr. Shupack."

"He wasn't a dwarf, Jason. I'm telling you. He was just short."

"Dr. T. is."

"He was just short, believe me."

"Uncle Bobby is," I tell her.

"Oh, fart on Uncle Bobby," my mother says. "Hamilton is not a dwarf, I promise you. He's just a little short."

The flight attendant says they don't have Dr Pepper.

My mom knows what to ask for next. I am already having trouble enough in this little seat because the man next to me is so close. He smells like BO or cheese. I have to turn off my smell button just so I can breathe.

"Sprite?"

"Why yes, ma'am. We do."

The snap of the can. The scoop of ice.

"Oh, no ice, please," my mother says. "Sorry."

"No problem, ma'am. Here you go, young man."

I like this lady and I like that my mom takes care of me and that I can take care of her. I think I can breathe very well now.

Just before the plane is going to land I can feel it tugging at the inside of my body. I can feel it pulling me down. I can feel the pressure inside my head and my stomach. The pilot tells us we are at a lower altitude and that we will be on the ground in twenty minutes. My mother told me my dad and Jeremy will be waiting at the airport.

I am excited.

I would like another Sprite, but the flight attendant is not here anymore.

"Jason?" my mother says to me. "I want to you know, this trip has been one of the best things I've ever done."

I hear her.

It's easy to listen with the wild drone of the airplane. It is like a giant vacuum that sucks up all the other noise. Nobody even hears when you pass gas out loud on a plane.

"All this time I thought I was supposed to be teaching you," my mother is saying to me. "I was wrong."

She takes a tissue out of her pocketbook.

"I thought you were supposed to learn how to get along without me." I know my mother is crying again. That kind of cry when she watches TV. It's not really sad. It won't last too long.

"But it was me, all along," she says. "It is me who needs you, Jason. You've taught me so much this trip. You've taught me about being brave."

I don't know what she is talking about. If my father were here, he wouldn't be doing this. He wouldn't be talking so much, or not at all, he sure wouldn't be crying, and that would be better. But it's okay. That's what my mom is like.

She can't help it.

We all have things we can't help doing.

Bennu's story has a kind of happy ending too.

Maybe not happy, so to speak, like happily ever after, but okay. Because I didn't want a sad ending. And I didn't want an unrealistic ending. And because life is kind of like that. You don't really know how it's going to end.

Hamilton told us that writing is a process. It doesn't always come out right the first time.

Right.

Write.

Right.

Like life, he said, but in writing you get to fix it. You get to rewrite. And rewrite and rewrite until you have the exact words you want.

So first thing when we get home, I turn on my computer and revise my story.

Bennu wakes up on the morning of his scheduled surgery, before the driver shows up to take him to the hospital. He lets his little feet hang off the edge of his bed, and he wiggles his toes. He takes a great big stretch and reaches his hands up to the sky. Then Bennu hops down and fixes himself a little breakfast, no pun intended. When he can't reach the toaster to get out his bread, his friend and roommate, Joshua, gets it for him.

He has a little trouble reaching the knobs in the shower, but he has a plastic stool he keeps in there, so he steps up onto it when he needs to turn the water on or off, or to adjust the temperature.

All the while Bennu is certain about what he is going to do about this surgery. He has made up his mind. After his shower Bennu dries off and then goes into his bedroom to take out the specially made clothes that fit his body. He pulls his belt an extra notch, and he takes one final look at himself in the mirror.

Then Bennu goes to the doctor's office and this is what he says:

Sorry, Doc. I changed my mind.

This is who I am.

This is me.

Nora Raleigh Baskin

has written several novels for middle-grade readers and teens, including *The Truth About My Bat Mitzvah, Basketball (Or Something Like It), In the Company of Crazies, Almost Home,* and her first book, *What Every Girl (Except Me) Knows,* for which she was chosen as a *Publishers Weekly* Flying Start. Nora lives with her family in Connecticut.